The Eagle's Shadow

The Eagle's Shadow

James Branch Cabell

MINT EDITIONS

The Eagle's Shadow was first published in 1904.

This edition published by Mint Editions 2020.

ISBN 9781513267616 | E-ISBN 9781513272610

Published by Mint Editions®

MINT
EDITIONS

minteditionbooks.com

Publishing Director: Jennifer Newens
Design & Production: Rachel Lopez Metzger
Typesetting: Westchester Publishing Services

The Characters

Colonel Thomas Hugonin, formerly in the service of Her Majesty the Empress of India, Margaret Hugonin's father.

Frederick R. Woods, the founder of Selwoode, Margaret's uncle by marriage.

Billy Woods, his nephew, Margaret's quondam fiancé.

Hugh Van Orden, a rather young young man, Margaret's adorer.

Martin Jeal, M.D., of Fairhaven, Margaret's family physician.

Cock-Eye Flinks, a gentleman of leisure, Margaret's chance acquaintance.

Petheridge Jukesbury, president of the Society for the Suppression of Nicotine and the Nude, Margaret's almoner in furthering the cause of education and temperance.

Felix Kennaston, a minor poet, Margaret's almoner in furthering the cause of literature and art.

Sarah Ellen Haggage, Madame President of the Ladies' League for the Edification of the Impecunious, Margaret's almoner in furthering the cause of charity and philanthropy. Kathleen Eppes Saumarez, a lecturer before women's clubs, Margaret's almoner in furthering the cause of theosophy, nature study, and rational dress.

Adèle Haggage, Mrs. Haggage's daughter, Margaret's rival with Hugh Van Orden.

And Margaret Hugonin.

The other participants in the story are Wilkins, Célestine, The Spring Moon and The Eagle.

Chapter 1

This is the story of Margaret Hugonin and of the Eagle. And with your permission, we will for the present defer all consideration of the bird, and devote our unqualified attention to Margaret.

I have always esteemed Margaret the obvious, sensible, most appropriate name that can be bestowed upon a girl-child, for it is a name that fits a woman—any woman—as neatly as her proper size in gloves.

Yes, the first point I wish to make is that a woman-child, once baptised Margaret, is thereby insured of a suitable name. Be she grave or gay in after-life, wanton or pious or sullen, comely or otherwise, there will be no possible chance of incongruity; whether she develop a taste for winter-gardens or the higher mathematics, whether she take to golf or clinging organdies, the event is provided for. One has only to consider for a moment, and if among a choice of Madge, Marjorie, Meta, Maggie, Margherita, Peggy, and Gretchen, and countless others—if among all these he cannot find a name that suits her to a T—why, then, the case is indeed desperate and he may permissibly fall back upon Madam or—if the cat jump propitiously, and at his own peril—on Darling or Sweetheart.

The second proof that this name must be the best of all possible names is that Margaret Hugonin bore it. And so the murder is out. You may suspect what you choose. I warn you in advance that I have no part whatever in her story; and if my admiration for her given name appear somewhat excessive, I can only protest that in this dissentient world every one has a right to his own taste. I knew Margaret. I admired her. And if in some unguarded moment I may have carried my admiration to the point of indiscretion, her husband most assuredly knows all about it, by this, and he and I are still the best of friends. So you perceive that if I ever did so far forget myself it could scarcely have amounted to a hanging matter.

I am doubly sure that Margaret Hugonin was beautiful, for the reason that I have never found a woman under forty-five who shared my opinion. If you clap a Testament into my hand, I cannot affirm that women are eager to recognise beauty in one another; at the utmost they concede that this or that particular feature is well enough. But when a woman is clean-eyed and straight-limbed, and has a cheery heart, she really cannot help being beautiful; and when Nature accords her a sufficiency of dimples and an infectious laugh, I protest she is well-nigh irresistible. And all these Margaret Hugonin had.

And surely that is enough.

I shall not endeavour, then, to picture her features to you in any nicely picked words. Her chief charm was that she was Margaret.

And besides that, mere carnal vanities are trivial things; a gray eye or so is not in the least to the purpose. Yet since it is the immemorial custom of writer-folk to inventory such possessions of their heroines, here you have a catalogue of her personal attractions. Launce's method will serve our turn.

Imprimis, there was not very much of her—five feet three, at the most; and hers was the well-groomed modern type that implies a grandfather or two and is in every respect the antithesis of that hulking Venus of the Louvre whom people pretend to admire. Item, she had blue eyes; and when she talked with you, her head drooped forward a little. The frank, intent gaze of these eyes was very flattering and, in its ultimate effect, perilous, since it led you fatuously to believe that she had forgotten there were any other trousered beings extant. Later on you found this a decided error. Item, she had a quite incredible amount of yellow hair, that was not in the least like gold or copper or bronze—I scorn the hackneyed similes of metallurgical poets—but a straightforward yellow, darkening at the roots; and she wore it low down on her neck in great coils that were held in place by a multitude of little golden hair-pins and divers corpulent tortoise-shell ones. Item, her nose was a tiny miracle of perfection; and this was noteworthy, for you will observe that Nature, who is an adept at eyes and hair and mouths, very rarely achieves a creditable nose. Item, she had a mouth; and if you are a Gradgrindian with a taste for hairsplitting, I cannot swear that it was a particularly small mouth. The lips were rather full than otherwise; one saw in them potentialities of heroic passion, and tenderness, and generosity, and, if you will, temper. No, her mouth was not in the least like the pink shoe-button of romance and sugared portraiture; it was manifestly designed less for simpering out of a gilt frame or the dribbling of stock phrases over three hundred pages than for gibes and laughter and cheery gossip and honest, unromantic eating, as well as another purpose, which, as a highly dangerous topic, I decline even to mention.

There you have the best description of Margaret Hugonin that I am capable of giving you. No one realises its glaring inadequacy more acutely than I.

Furthermore, I stipulate that if in the progress of our comedy she appear to act with an utter lack of reason or even common-sense—as every woman worth the winning must do once or twice in a lifetime—that I be permitted to record the fact, to set it down in all its ugliness, nay, even to exaggerate it a little—all to the end that I may eventually exasperate you and goad you into crying out, "Come, come, you are not treating the girl with common justice!"

For, if such a thing were possible, I should desire you to rival even me in a liking for Margaret Hugonin. And speaking for myself, I can assure you that I have come long ago to regard her faults with the same leniency that I accord my own.

Chapter 2

We begin on a fine May morning in Colonel Hugonin's rooms at Selwoode, which is, as you may or may not know, the Hugonins' country-place. And there we discover the Colonel dawdling over his breakfast, in an intermediate stage of that careful toilet which enables him later in the day to pass casual inspection as turning forty-nine.

At present the old gentleman is discussing the members of his daughter's house-party. We will omit, by your leave, a number of picturesque descriptive passages—for the Colonel is, on occasion, a man of unfettered speech—and come hastily to the conclusion, to the summing-up of the whole matter.

"Altogether," says Colonel Hugonin, "they strike me as being the most ungodly menagerie ever gotten together under one roof since Noah landed on Ararat."

Now, I am sorry that veracity compels me to present the Colonel in this particular state of mind, for ordinarily he was as pleasant-spoken a gentleman as you will be apt to meet on the longest summer day.

You must make allowances for the fact that, on this especial morning, he was still suffering from a recent twinge of the gout, and that his toast was somewhat dryer than he liked it; and, most potent of all, that the foreign mail, just in, had caused him to rebel anew against the proprieties and his daughter's inclinations, which chained him to Selwoode, in the height of the full London season, to preside over a house-party every member of which he cordially disliked. Therefore, the Colonel having glanced through the well-known names of those at Lady Pevensey's last cotillion, groaned and glared at his daughter, who sat opposite him, and reviled his daughter's friends with point and fluency, and characterised them as above, for the reason that he was hungered at heart for the shady side of Pall Mall, and that their presence at Selwoode prevented his attaining this Elysium. For, I am sorry to say that the Colonel loathed all things American, saving his daughter, whom he worshipped.

And, I think, no one who could have seen her preparing his second cup of tea would have disputed that in making this exception he acted with a show of reason. For Margaret Hugonin—but, as you know, she is our heroine, and, as I fear you have already learned, words are very paltry makeshifts when it comes to describing her. Let us simply say, then, that Margaret, his daughter, began to make him a cup of tea, and add that she laughed.

Not unkindly; no, for at bottom she adored her father—a comely Englishman of some sixty-odd, who had run through his wife's fortune and his own, in the most gallant fashion—and she accorded his opinions a conscientious, but at times, a sorely taxed, tolerance. That very month she had reached twenty-three, the age of omniscience, when the fallacies and general obtuseness of older people become dishearteningly apparent.

"It's nonsense," pursued the old gentleman, "utter, bedlamite nonsense, filling Selwoode up with writing people! Never heard of such a thing. Gad, I do remember, as a young man, meeting Thackeray at a garden-party at Orleans House—gentlemanly fellow with a broken nose—and Browning went about a bit, too, now I think of it. People had 'em one at a time to lend flavour to a dinner—like an olive; we didn't dine on olives, though. You have 'em for breakfast, luncheon, dinner, and everything! I'm sick of olives, I tell you, Margaret!" Margaret pouted.

"They ain't even good olives. I looked into one of that fellow Charteris's books the other day—that chap you had here last week. It was bally rot—proverbs standing on their heads and grinning like dwarfs in a condemned street-fair! Who wants to be told that impropriety is the spice of life and that a roving eye gathers remorse? *You* may call that sort of thing cleverness, if you like; I call it damn' foolishness." And the emphasis with which he said this left no doubt that the Colonel spoke his honest opinion.

"Attractive," said his daughter patiently, "Mr. Charteris is very, very clever. Mr. Kennaston says literature suffered a considerable loss when he began to write for the magazines."

And now that Margaret has spoken, permit me to call your attention to her voice. Mellow and suave and of astonishing volume was Margaret's voice; it came not from the back of her throat, as most of our women's voices do, but from her chest; and I protest it had the timbre of a violin. Men, hearing her voice for the first time, were wont to stare at her a little and afterward to close their hands slowly, for always its modulations had the tonic sadness of distant music, and it thrilled you to much the same magnanimity and yearning, cloudily conceived; and yet you could not but smile in spite of yourself at the quaint emphasis fluttering through her speech and pouncing for the most part on the unlikeliest word in the whole sentence.

But I fancy the Colonel must have been tone-deaf. "Don't you make phrases for me!" he snorted; "you keep 'em for your menagerie Think! By gad, the world never thinks. I believe the world deliberately reads the six bestselling books in order to incapacitate itself for thinking." Then, his wrath gathering emphasis as he went on: "The longer I live the plainer I see Shakespeare was right—what fools these mortals be, and all that. There's that Haggage woman—speech-making through the country like a hiatused politician. It may be philanthropic, but it ain't ladylike—no, begad! What has she got to do with Juvenile Courts and child-labour in the South, I'd like to know? Why ain't she at home attending to that crippled boy of hers—poor little beggar!—instead of flaunting through America meddling with other folk's children?"

Miss Hugonin put another lump of sugar into his cup and deigned no reply.

"By gad," cried the Colonel fervently, "if you're so anxious to spend that money of yours in charity, why don't you found a Day Nursery for the Children of Philanthropists—a place where advanced men and women can leave their offspring in capable hands when they're busied with Mothers' Meetings and Educational Conferences? It would do a thousand times more good, I can tell you, than that fresh kindergarten scheme of yours for teaching the children of the labouring classes to make a new sort of mud-pie."

"You don't understand these things, attractive," Margaret gently pointed out. "You aren't in harmony with the trend of modern thought."

"No, thank God!" said the Colonel, heartily.

Ensued a silence during which he chipped at his egg-shell in an absent-minded fashion.

"That fellow Kennaston said anything to you yet?" he presently queried.

"I—I don't understand," she protested—oh, perfectly unconvincingly. The tea-making, too, engrossed her at this point to an utterly improbable extent.

Thus it shortly befell that the Colonel, still regarding her under intent brows, cleared his throat and made bold to question her generosity in the matter of sugar; five lumps being, as he suggested, a rather unusual allowance for one cup.

Then, "Mr. Kennaston and I are very good friends," said she, with dignity. And having spoiled the first cup in the making, she began on another.

"Glad to hear it," growled the old gentleman. "I hope you value his friendship sufficiently not to marry him. The man's a fraud—a flimsy, sickening fraud, like his poetry, begad, and that's made up of botany and wide margins and indecency in about equal proportions. It ain't fit for a woman to read—in fact, a woman ought not to read anything; a comprehension of the Decalogue and the cookery-book is enough learning for the best of 'em. Your mother never—never—"

Colonel Hugonin paused and stared at the open window for a little. He seemed to be interested in something a great way off.

"We used to read Ouida's books together," he said, somewhat wistfully. "Lord, Lord, how she revelled in Chandos and Bertie Cecil and those dashing Life Guardsmen! And she used to toss that little head of hers and say I was a finer figure of a man than any of 'em—thirty years ago, good Lord! And I was then, but I ain't now. I'm only a broken-down, cantankerous old fool," declared the Colonel, blowing his nose violently, "and that's why I'm quarrelling with the dearest, foolishest daughter man ever had. Ah, my dear, don't mind me—run your menagerie as you like, and I'll stand it."

Margaret adopted her usual tactics; she perched herself on the arm of his chair and began to stroke his cheek very gently. She often wondered as to what dear sort of a woman that tender-eyed, pink-cheeked mother of the old miniature had been—the mother who had died when she was two years old. She loved the idea of her, vague as it was. And, just now, somehow, the notion of two grown people reading Ouida did not strike her as being especially ridiculous.

"Was she very beautiful?" she asked, softly.

"My dear," said her father, "you are the picture of her."

"You dangerous old man!" said she, laughing and rubbing her cheek against his in a manner that must have been highly agreeable. "Dear, do you know that is the nicest little compliment I've had for a long time?"

Thereupon the Colonel chuckled. "Pay me for it, then," said he, "by driving the dog-cart over to meet Billy's train to-day. Eh?"

"I—I can't," said Miss Hugonin, promptly.

"Why?" demanded her father.

"Because——" said Miss Hugonin; and after giving this really excellent reason, reflected for a moment and strengthened it by adding, "Because——"

"See here," her father questioned, "what did you two quarrel about, anyway?"

"I—I really don't remember," said she, reflectively; then continued, with hauteur and some inconsistency, "I am not aware that Mr. Woods and I have ever quarrelled."

"By gad, then," said the Colonel, "you may as well prepare to, for I intend to marry you to Billy some day. Dear, dear, child," he interpolated, with malice aforethought, "have you a fever?—your cheek's like a coal. Billy's a man, I tell you—worth a dozen of your Kennastons and Charterises. I like Billy. And besides, it's only right he should have Selwoode—wasn't he brought up to expect it? It ain't right he should lose it simply because he had a quarrel with Frederick, for, by gad—not to speak unkindly of the dead, my dear—Frederick quarrelled with every one he ever knew, from the woman who nursed him to the doctor who gave him his last pill. He may have gotten his genius for money-making from Heaven, but he certainly got his temper from the devil. I really believe," said the Colonel, reflectively, "it was worse than mine. Yes, not a doubt of it—I'm a lamb in comparison. But he had his way, after all; and even now poor Billy can't get Selwoode without taking you with it," and he caught his daughter's face between his hands and turned it toward his for a moment. "I wonder now," said he, in meditative wise, "if Billy will consider that a drawback?"

It seemed very improbable. Any number of marriageable males would have sworn it was unthinkable.

However, "Of course," Margaret began, in a crisp voice, "if you advise Mr. Woods to marry me as a good speculation—"

But her father caught her up, with a whistle. "Eh?" said he. "Love in a cottage?—is it thus the poet turns his lay? That's damn' nonsense! I tell you, even in a cottage the plumber's bill has to be paid, and the grocer's little account settled every month. Yes, by gad, and even if you elect to live on bread and cheese and kisses, you'll find Camembert a bit more to your taste than Sweitzer."

"But I don't want to marry anybody, you ridiculous old dear," said Margaret.

"Oh, very well," said the old gentleman; "don't. Be an old maid, and lecture before the Mothers' Club, if you like. I don't care. Anyhow, you meet Billy to-day at twelve-forty-five. You will?—that's a good child. Now run along and tell the menagerie I'll be down-stairs as soon as I've finished dressing."

And the Colonel rang for his man and proceeded to finish his toilet. He seemed a thought absent-minded this morning.

"I say, Wilkins," he questioned, after a little. "Ever read any of Ouida's books?"

"Ho, yes, sir," said Wilkins; "Miss 'Enderson—Mrs. 'Aggage's maid, that his, sir—was reading haloud hout hof 'Hunder Two Flags' honly last hevening, sir."

"H'm—Wilkins—if you can run across one of them in the servants' quarters—you might leave it—by my bed—to-night."

"Yes, sir."

"And—h'm, Wilkins—you can put it under that book of Herbert Spencer's my daughter gave me yesterday. *Under* it, Wilkins—and, h'm, Wilkins—you needn't mention it to anybody. Ouida ain't cultured, Wilkins, but she's damn' good reading. I suppose that's why she ain't cultured, Wilkins."

Chapter 3

And now let us go back a little. In a word, let us utilise the next twenty minutes—during which Miss Hugonin drives to the neighbouring railway station, in, if you press me, not the most pleasant state of mind conceivable—by explaining a thought more fully the posture of affairs at Selwoode on the May morning that starts our story.

And to do this I must commence with the nature of the man who founded Selwoode.

It was when the nineteenth century was still a hearty octogenarian that Frederick R. Woods caused Selwoode to be builded. I give you the name by which he was known on "the Street." A mythology has grown about the name since, and strange legends of its owner are still narrated where brokers congregate. But with the lambs he sheared, and the bulls he dragged to earth, and the bears he gored to financial death, we have nothing to do; suffice it, that he performed these operations with almost uniform success and in an unimpeachably respectable manner.

And if, in his time, he added materially to the lists of inmates in various asylums and almshouses, it must be acknowledged that he bore his victims no malice, and that on every Sunday morning he confessed himself to be a miserable sinner, in a voice that was perfectly audible three pews off. At bottom, I think he considered his relations with Heaven on a purely business basis; he kept a species of running account with Providence; and if on occasions he overdrew it somewhat, he saw no incongruity in evening matters with a cheque for the church fund.

So that at his death it was said of him that he had, in his day, sent more men into bankruptcy and more missionaries into Africa than any other man in the country.

In his sixty-fifth year, he caught Alfred Van Orden short in Lard, erected a memorial window to his wife and became a country gentleman. He never set foot in Wall Street again. He builded Selwoode—a handsome Tudor manor which stands some seven miles from the village of Fairhaven—where he dwelt in state, by turns affable and domineering to the neighbouring farmers, and evincing a grave interest in the condition of their crops. He no longer turned to the financial reports in the papers; and the pedigree of the Woodses hung in the living-hall for all men to see, beginning gloriously with Woden, the

Scandinavian god, and attaining a respectable culmination in the names of Frederick R. Woods and of William, his brother.

It is not to be supposed that he omitted to supply himself with a coat-of-arms. Frederick R. Woods evinced an almost childlike pride in his heraldic blazonings.

"The Woods arms," he would inform you, with a relishing gusto, "are vert, an eagle displayed, barry argent and gules. And the crest is out of a ducal coronet, or, a demi-eagle proper. We have no motto, sir—none of your ancient coats have mottoes."

The Woods Eagle he gloried in. The bird was perched in every available nook at Selwoode; it was carved in the woodwork, was set in the mosaics, was chased in the tableware, was woven in the napery, was glazed in the very china. Turn where you would, an eagle or two confronted you; and Hunston Wyke, who is accounted something of a wit, swore that Frederick R. Woods at Selwoode reminded him of "a sore-headed bear who had taken up permanent quarters in an aviary."

There was one, however, who found the bear no very untractable monster. This was the son of his brother, dead now, who dwelt at Selwoode as heir presumptive. Frederick R. Woods's wife had died long ago, leaving him childless. His brother's boy was an orphan; and so, for a time, he and the grim old man lived together peaceably enough. Indeed, Billy Woods was in those days as fine a lad as you would wish to see, with the eyes of an inquisitive cherub and a big tow-head, which Frederick R. Woods fell into the habit of cuffing heartily, in order to conceal the fact that he would have burned Selwoode to the ground rather than allow any one else to injure a hair of it.

In the consummation of time, Billy, having attained the ripe age of eighteen, announced to his uncle that he intended to become a famous painter. Frederick R. Woods exhorted him not to be a fool, and packed him off to college.

Billy Woods returned on his first vacation with a fragmentary mustache and any quantity of paint-tubes, canvases, palettes, mahl-sticks, and suchlike paraphernalia. Frederick R. Woods passed over the mustache, and had the painters' trappings burned by the second footman. Billy promptly purchased another lot. His uncle came upon them one morning, rubbed his chin meditatively for a moment, and laughed for the first time, so far as known, in his lifetime; then he tiptoed to his own apartments, lest Billy— the lazy young rascal was still abed in the next room—should awaken and discover his knowledge of this act of flat rebellion.

I dare say the old gentleman was so completely accustomed to having his own way that this unlooked-for opposition tickled him by its novelty; or perhaps he recognised in Billy an obstinacy akin to his own; or perhaps it was merely that he loved the boy. In any event, he never again alluded to the subject; and it is a fact that when Billy sent for carpenters to convert an upper room into an atelier, Frederick R. Woods spent two long and dreary weeks in Boston in order to remain in ignorance of the entire affair.

Billy scrambled through college, somehow, in the allotted four years. At the end of that time, he returned to find new inmates installed at Selwoode.

For the wife of Frederick R. Woods had been before her marriage one of the beautiful Anstruther sisters, who, as certain New Yorkers still remember—those grizzled, portly, rosy-gilled fellows who prattle on provocation of Jenny Lind and Castle Garden, and remember everything—created a pronounced furor at their début in the days of crinoline and the Grecian bend; and Margaret Anstruther, as they will tell you, was married to Thomas Hugonin, then a gallant cavalry officer in the service of Her Majesty, the Empress of India.

And she must have been the nicer of the two, because everybody who knew her says that Margaret Hugonin is exactly like her.

So it came about naturally enough, that Billy Woods, now an *Artium Baccalaureus*, if you please, and not a little proud of it, found the Colonel and his daughter, then on a visit to this country, installed at Selwoode as guests and quasi-relatives. And Billy was twenty-two, and Margaret was nineteen.

PRECISELY WHAT HAPPENED I AM unable to tell you. Billy Woods claims it is none of my business; and Margaret says that it was a long, long time ago and she really can't remember.

But I fancy we can all form a very fair notion of what is most likely to occur when two sensible, normal, healthy young people are thrown together in this intimate fashion at a country-house where the remaining company consists of two elderly gentlemen. Billy was forced to be polite to his uncle's guest; and Margaret couldn't well be discourteous to her host's nephew, could she? Of course not: so it befell in the course of time that Frederick R. Woods and the Colonel—who had quickly become a great favourite, by virtue of his implicit faith in the Eagle and in Woden and Sir Percival de Wode of Hastings, and such-like flights of heraldic fancy, and had augmented his popularity by his really brilliant suggestion of Wynkyn de Worde, the famous sixteenth-century printer, as a probable collateral relation of the family—it came to pass, I say, that the two gentlemen nodded over their port and chuckled, and winked at one another and agreed that the thing would do.

This was all very well; but they failed to make allowances for the inevitable quarrel and the subsequent spectacle of the gentleman contemplating suicide and the lady looking wistfully toward a nunnery. In this case it arose, I believe, over Teddy Anstruther, who for a cousin was undeniably very attentive to Margaret; and in the natural course of events they would have made it up before the week was out had not Frederick R. Woods selected this very moment to interfere in the matter.

Ah, *si vieillesse savait!*

The blundering old man summoned Billy into his study and ordered him to marry Margaret Hugonin, precisely as the Colonel might have ordered a private to go on sentry-duty. Ten days earlier Billy would have jumped at the chance; ten days later he would probably have suggested it himself; but at that exact moment he would have as willingly contemplated matrimony with Alecto or Medusa or any of the Furies. Accordingly, he declined. Frederick R. Woods flew into a pyrotechnical display of temper, and gave him his choice between obeying his commands and leaving his house forever—the choice, in fact, which he had been according Billy at very brief intervals ever since the boy had had the measles, fifteen years before, and had refused to take the proper medicines.

It was merely his usual manner of expressing a request or a suggestion. But this time, to his utter horror and amaze, the boy took him at his word and left Selwoode within the hour.

Billy's life, you see, was irrevocably blighted. It mattered very little what became of him; personally, he didn't care in the least. But as for that fair, false, fickle woman—perish the thought! Sooner a thousand deaths! No, he would go to Paris and become a painter of worldwide reputation; the money his father had left him would easily suffice for his simple wants. And some day, the observed of all observers in some bright hall of gaiety, he would pass her coldly by, with a cynical smile upon his lips, and she would grow pale and totter and fall into the arms of the bloated Silenus, for whose title she had bartered her purely superficial charms.

Yes, upon mature deliberation, that was precisely what Billy decided to do.

Followed dark days at Selwoode. Frederick R. Woods told Margaret of what had occurred; and he added the information that, as his wife's nearest relative, he intended to make her his heir.

Then Margaret did what I would scarcely have expected of Margaret. She turned upon him like a virago and informed Frederick R. Woods precisely what she thought of him; she acquainted him with the fact that he was a sordid, low-minded, grasping beast, and a miser, and a tyrant, and (I think) a parricide; she notified him that he was thoroughly unworthy to wipe the dust off his nephew's shoes—an office toward which, to do him justice, he had never shown any marked aspirations—and that Billy had acted throughout in a most noble and sensible manner; and that, personally, she wouldn't marry Billy Woods if he were the last man on earth, for she had always despised him; and she added the information that she expected to die shortly, and she hoped they would both be sorry *then*; and subsequently she clapped the climax by throwing her arms about his neck and bursting into tears and telling him he was the dearest old man in the world and that she was thoroughly ashamed of herself.

So they kissed and made it up. And after a little the Colonel and Margaret went away from Selwoode, and Frederick R. Woods was left alone to nourish his anger and indignation, if he could, and to hunger for his boy, whether he would or not. He was too proud to seek him out; indeed, he never thought of that; and so he waited alone in his fine house, sick at heart, impotent, hoping against hope that the boy would come back. The boy never came.

No, the boy never came, because he was what the old man had made him—headstrong, and wilful, and obstinate. Billy had been thoroughly spoiled. The old man had nurtured his pride, had applauded it as a mark of proper spirit; and now it was this same pride that had robbed him of the one thing he loved in all the world.

So, at last, the weak point in the armour of this sturdy old Pharisee was found, and Fate had pierced it gaily. It was retribution, if you will; and I think that none of his victims in "the Street," none of the countless widows and orphans that he had made, suffered more bitterly than he in those last days.

It was almost two years after Billy's departure from Selwoode that his body-servant, coming to rouse Frederick R. Woods one June morning, found him dead in his rooms. He had been ailing for some time. It was his heart, the doctors said; and I think that it was, though not precisely in the sense which they meant.

JAMES BRANCH CABELL

The man found him seated before his great carved desk, on which his head and shoulders had fallen forward; they rested on a sheet of legal-cap paper half-covered with a calculation in his crabbed old hand as to the value of certain properties—the calculation which he never finished; and underneath was a mass of miscellaneous papers, among them his will, dated the day after Billy left Selwoode, in which Frederick R. Woods bequeathed his millions unconditionally to Margaret Hugonin when she should come of age.

Her twenty-first birthday had fallen in the preceding month. So Margaret was one of the richest women in America; and you may depend upon it, that if many men had loved her before, they worshipped her now—or, at least, said they did, and, after all, their protestations were the only means she had of judging. She might have been a countess—and it must be owned that the old Colonel, who had an honest Anglo-Saxon reverence for a title, saw this chance lost wistfully—and she might have married any number of grammarless gentlemen, personally unknown to her, whose fervent proposals almost every mail brought in; and besides these, there were many others, more orthodox in their wooing, some of whom were genuinely in love with Margaret Hugonin, and some—I grieve to admit it—who were genuinely in love with her money; and she would have none of them.

She refused them all with the utmost civility, as I happen to know. How I learned it is no affair of yours.

For Miss Hugonin had remarkably keen eyes, which she used to advantage. In the world about her they discovered very little that she could admire. She was none the happier for her wealth; the piled-up millions overshadowed her personality; and it was not long before she knew that most people regarded her simply as the heiress of the Woods fortune—an unavoidable encumbrance attached to the property, which divers thrifty-minded gentlemen were willing to put up with. To put up with!—at the thought, her pride rose in a hot blush, and, it must be confessed, she sought consolation in the looking-glass.

She was an humble-minded young woman, as the sex goes, and she saw no great reason there why a man should go mad over Margaret Hugonin. This decision, I grant you, was preposterous, for there were any number of reasons. Her final conclusion, however, was for the future to regard all men as fortune-hunters and to do her hair differently.

She carried out both resolutions. When a gentleman grew pressing in his attentions, she more than suspected his motives; and when she eventually declined him it was done with perfect, courtesy, but the glow of her eyes was at such times accentuated to a marked degree.

Meanwhile, the Eagle brooded undisturbed at Selwoode. Miss Hugonin would allow nothing to be altered.

"The place doesn't belong to me, attractive," she would tell her father. "I belong to the place. Yes, I do—I'm exactly like a little cow thrown in with a little farm when they sell it, and *all* my little suitors think so, and they are very willing to take me on those terms, too. But they shan't, attractive. I hate every single solitary man in the whole wide world but you, beautiful, and I particularly hate that horrid old Eagle; but we'll keep him because he's a constant reminder to me that Solomon or Moses, or whoever it was that said all men were liars, was a person of *very* great intelligence."

So that I think we may fairly say the money did her no good.

If it benefited no one else, it was not Margaret's fault. She had a high sense of her responsibilities, and therefore, at various times, endeavoured to further the spread of philanthropy and literature and theosophy and art and temperance and education and other laudable causes. Mr. Kennaston, in his laughing manner, was wont to jest at her varied enterprises and term her Lady Bountiful; but, then, Mr. Kennaston had no real conception of the proper uses of money. In fact, he never thought of money. He admitted this to Margaret with a whimsical sigh.

Margaret grew very fond of Mr. Kennaston because he was not mercenary.

Mr. Kennaston was much at Selwoode. Many people came there now—masculine women and muscleless men, for the most part. They had, every one of them, some scheme for bettering the universe; and if among them Margaret seemed somewhat out of place—a butterfly among earnest-minded ants—her heart was in every plan they advocated, and they found her purse-strings infinitely elastic. The girl was pitiably anxious to be of some use in the world.

So at Selwoode they gossiped of great causes and furthered the millenium. And above them the Eagle brooded in silence.

And Billy? All this time Billy was junketing abroad, where every year he painted masterpieces for the Salon, which—on account of a nefarious conspiracy among certain artists, jealous of his superior merits—were invariably refused.

Now Billy is back again in America, and the Colonel has insisted that he come to Selwoode, and Margaret is waiting for him in the dog-cart.

The glow of her eyes is very, very bright. Her father's careless words this morning, coupled with certain speeches of Mr. Kennaston's last night, have given her food for reflection.

"He wouldn't dare," says Margaret, to no one in particular. "Oh, no, he wouldn't dare after what happened four years ago."

And, Margaret-like, she has quite forgotten that what happened four years ago was all caused by her having flirted outrageously with Teddy Anstruther, in order to see what Billy would do.

Chapter 4

T he twelve forty-five, for a wonder, was on time; and there descended from it a big, blond young man, who did not look in the least like a fortune-hunter.

Miss Hugonin resented this. Manifestly, he looked clean and honest for the deliberate purpose of deceiving her. Very well! She'd show him!

He was quite unembarrassed. He shook hands cordially; then he shook hands with the groom, who, you may believe it, was grinning in a most unprofessional manner because Master Billy was back again at Selwoode. Subsequently, in his old decisive way, he announced they would walk to the house, as his legs needed stretching.

The insolence of it!—quite as if he had something to say to Margaret in private and couldn't wait a minute. Beyond doubt, this was a young man who must be taken down a peg or two, and that at once. Of course, she wasn't going to walk back with him!—a pretty figure they'd cut strolling through the fields, like a house-girl and the milkman on a Sunday afternoon! She would simply say she was too tired to walk, and that would end the matter.

So she said she thought the exercise would do them both good.

They came presently with desultory chat to a meadow bravely decked in all the gauds of Spring. About them the day was clear, the air bland. Spring had revamped her ageless fripperies of tender leaves and bird-cries and sweet, warm odours for the adornment of this meadow; above it she had set a turkis sky splashed here and there with little clouds that were like whipped cream; and upon it she had scattered largesse, a Danaë's shower of buttercups. Altogether, she had made of it a particularly dangerous meadow for a man and a maid to frequent.

Yet there Mr. Woods paused under a burgeoning maple—paused resolutely, with the lures of Spring thick about him, compassed with every snare of scent and sound and colour that the witch is mistress of.

Margaret hoped he had a pleasant passage over. Her father, thank you, was in the pink of condition. Oh, yes, she was quite well. She hoped Mr. Woods would not find America—

"Well, Peggy," said Mr. Woods, "then, we'll have it out right here."

His insolence was so surprising that—in order to recover herself—Margaret actually sat down under the maple-tree. Peggy, indeed! Why, she hadn't been called Peggy for—no, not for four whole years!

"Because I intend to be friends, you know," said Mr. Woods.

And about them the maple-leaves made a little island of sombre green, around which more vivid grasses rippled and dimpled under the fitful spring breezes. And everywhere leaves lisped to one another, and birds shrilled insistently. It was a perilous locality.

I fancy Billy Woods was out of his head when he suggested being friends in such a place. Friends, indeed!—you would have thought from the airy confidence with which he spoke that Margaret had come safely to forty year and wore steel-rimmed spectacles!

But Miss Hugonin merely cast down her eyes and was aware of no reason why they shouldn't be. She was sure he must be hungry, and she thought luncheon must be ready by now.

In his soul, Mr. Woods observed that her lashes were long—long beyond all reason. Lacking the numbers that Petrarch flowed in, he did not venture, even to himself, to characterise them further. But oh, how queer it was they should be pure gold at the roots!—she must have dipped them in the ink-pot. And oh, the strong, sudden, bewildering curve of 'em! He could not recall at the present moment ever noticing quite such lashes anywhere else. No, it was highly improbable that there were such lashes anywhere else. Perhaps a few of the superior angels might have such lashes. He resolved for the future to attend church more regularly.

Aloud, Mr. Woods observed that in that case they had better shake hands.

It would have been ridiculous to contest the point. The dignified course was to shake hands, since he insisted on it, and then to return at once to Selwoode.

Margaret Hugonin had a pretty hand, and Mr. Woods, as an artist, could not well fail to admire it. Still, he needn't have looked at it as though he had never before seen anything quite like it; he needn't have neglected to return it; and when Miss Hugonin reclaimed it, after a decent interval, he needn't have laughed in a manner that compelled her to laugh, too. These things were unnecessary and annoying, as they caused Margaret to forget that she despised him.

For the time being—will you believe it?—she actually thought he was rather nice.

"I acted like an ass," said Mr. Woods, tragically. "Oh, yes, I did, you know. But if you'll forgive me for having been an ass I'll forgive you for throwing me over for Teddy Anstruther, and at the wedding I'll dance through any number of pairs of patent-leathers you choose to mention."

So that was the way he looked at it. Teddy Anstruther, indeed! Why, Teddy was a dark little man with brown eyes—just the sort of man she most objected to. How could any one ever possibly fancy a brown-eyed man? Then, for no apparent reason, Margaret flushed, and Billy, who had stretched his great length of limb on the grass beside her, noted it with a pair of the bluest eyes in the world and thought it vastly becoming.

"Billy," said she, impulsively—and the name having slipped out once by accident, it would have been absurd to call him anything else afterward—"it was horrid of you to refuse to take any of that money."

"But I didn't want it," he protested. "Good Lord, I'd only have done something foolish with it. It was awfully square of you, Peggy, to offer to divide, but I didn't want it, you see. I don't want to be a millionaire, and give up the rest of my life to founding libraries and explaining to people that if they never spend any money on amusements they'll have a great deal by the time they're too old to enjoy it. I'd rather paint pictures."

So that I think Margaret must have endeavoured at some time to make him accept part of Frederick R. Woods's money.

"You make me feel—and look—like a thief," she reproved him.

Then Billy laughed a little. "You don't look in the least like one," he reassured her. "You look like an uncommonly honest, straightforward young woman," Mr. Woods added, handsomely, "and I don't believe you'd purloin under the severest temptation."

She thanked him for his testimonial, with all three dimples in evidence.

This was unsettling. He hedged.

"Except, perhaps—" said he.

"Yes?" queried Margaret, after a pause.

However, she questioned him with her head drooped forward, her brows raised; and as this gave him the full effect of her eyes, Mr. Woods became quite certain that there was, at least, one thing she might be expected to rob him of, and wisely declined to mention it.

Margaret did not insist on knowing what it was. Perhaps she heard it thumping under his waistcoat, where it was behaving very queerly.

So they sat in silence for a while. Then Margaret fell a-humming to herself; and the air—will you believe it?—chanced by the purest accident to be that foolish, senseless old song they used to sing together four years ago.

Billy chuckled. "Let's!" he obscurely pleaded.

Spring prompted her.

JAMES BRANCH CABELL

> *"Oh, where have you been, Billy boy?"*
> *queried Margaret's wonderful contralto,*
>
> *"Oh, where have you been, Billy boy, Billy boy?*
> *Oh, where have you been, charming Billy?"*

She sang it in a low, hushed voice, just over her breath. Not looking at him, however. And oh, what a voice! thought Billy Woods. A voice that was honey and gold and velvet and all that is most sweet and rich and soft in the world! Find me another voice like that, you *prime donne!* Find me a simile for it, you uninventive poets! Indeed, I'd like to see you do it.

But he chimed in, nevertheless, with his pleasant throaty baritone, and lilted his own part quite creditably.

> *"I've been to seek a wife,*
> *She's the joy of my life;*
> *She's a young thing, and cannot leave her mother"*—

Only Billy sang it "father," just as they used to do.

And then they sang it through, did Margaret and Billy—sang of the dimple in her chin and the ringlets in her hair, and of the cherry pies she achieved with such celerity—sang as they sat in the spring-decked meadow every word of that inane old song that is so utterly senseless and so utterly unforgettable.

It was a quite idiotic performance. I set it down to the snares of Spring—to her insidious, delightful snares of scent and sound and colour that—for the moment, at least—had trapped these young people into loving life infinitely.

But I wonder who is responsible for that tatter of rhyme and melody that had come to them from nowhere in particular? Mr. Woods, as he sat up at the conclusion of the singing vigorously to applaud, would have shared his last possession, his ultimate crust, with that unknown benefactor of mankind. Indeed, though, the heart of Mr. Woods just now was full of loving kindness and capable of any freakish magnanimity.

For—will it be believed?—Mr. Woods, who four years ago had thrown over a fortune and exiled himself from his native land, rather than propose marriage to Margaret Hugonin, had no sooner come again into her presence and looked once into her perfectly fathomless eyes than he could no more have left her of his own accord than a moth can turn his back to a lighted candle. He had fancied himself entirely cured of that boy-and-girl nonsense; his broken heart, after the first few months, had not interfered in the least with a naturally healthy appetite; and, behold, here was the old malady raging again in his veins and with renewed fervour.

And all because the girl had a pretty face! I think you will agree with me that in the conversation I have recorded Margaret had not displayed any great wisdom or learning or tenderness or wit, nor, in fine, any of the qualities a man might naturally look for in a helpmate. Yet at the precise moment he handed his baggage-check to the groom, Mr. Woods had made up his mind to marry her. In an instant he had fallen head over ears in love; or to whittle accuracy to a point, he had discovered that he had never fallen out of love; and if you had offered him an empress or fetched Helen of Troy from the grave for his delectation he would have laughed you to scorn.

In his defense, I can only plead that Margaret was an unusually beautiful woman. It is all very well to flourish a death's-head at the feast, and bid my lady go paint herself an inch thick, for to this favour she must come; and it is quite true that the reddest lips in the universe may give vent to slander and lies, and the brightest eyes be set in the dullest head, and the most roseate of complexions be purchased at the corner drug-store; but, say what you will, a pretty woman is a pretty woman, and while she continue so no amount of common-sense or experience will prevent a man, on provocation, from alluring, coaxing, even entreating her to make a fool of him. We like it. And I think they like it, too.

So Mr. Woods lost his heart on a fine spring morning and was unreasonably elated over the fact.

And Margaret? Margaret was content.

Chapter 5

They talked for a matter of a half-hour in the fashion aforetime recorded—not very wise nor witty talk, if you will, but very pleasant to make. There were many pauses. There was much laughter over nothing in particular. There were any number of sentences ambitiously begun that ended nowhere. Altogether, it was just the sort of talk for a man and a maid.

Yet some twenty minutes later, Mr. Woods, preparing for luncheon in the privacy of his chamber, gave a sudden exclamation. Then he sat down and rumpled his hair thoroughly.

"Good Lord!" he groaned; "I'd forgotten all about that damned money! Oh, you ass!—you abject ass! Why, she's one of the richest women in America, and you're only a fifth-rate painter with a paltry thousand or so a year! *You* marry her!—why, I dare say she's refused a hundred better men than you! She'd think you were mad! Why, she'd think you were after her money! She—oh, she'd only think you a precious cheeky ass, she would, and she'd be quite right. You *are* an ass, Billy Woods! You ought to be locked up in some nice quiet stable, where your heehawing wouldn't disturb people. You need a keeper, you do!"

He sat for some ten minutes, aghast. Afterward he rose and threw back his shoulders and drew a deep breath.

"No, we aren't an ass," he addressed his reflection in the mirror, as he carefully knotted his tie. "We're only a poor chuckle-headed moth who's been looking at a star too long. It's a bright star, Billy, but it isn't for you. So we're going to be sensible now. We're going to get a telegram to-morrow that will call us away from Selwoode. We aren't coming back any more, either. We're simply going to continue painting fifth-rate pictures, and hoping that some day she'll find the right man and be very, very happy."

Nevertheless, he decided that a blue tie would look better, and was very particular in arranging it.

At the same moment Margaret stood before her mirror and tidied her hair for luncheon and assured her image in the glass that she was a weak-minded fool. She pointed out to herself the undeniable fact that Billy, having formerly refused to marry her—oh, ignominy!—seemed pleasant-spoken enough, now that she had become an heiress. His refusal to accept part of her fortune was a very flimsy device; it simply meant he hoped to get all of it. Oh, he did, did he!

Margaret powdered her nose viciously.

She saw through him! His honest bearing she very plainly perceived to be the result of consummate hypocrisy. In his laughter her keen ear detected a hollow ring; and his courteous manner she found, at bottom, mere servility. And finally she demonstrated—to her own satisfaction, at least—that his charm of manner was of exactly the, same sort that had been possessed by many other eminently distinguished criminals.

How did she do this? My dear sir, you had best inquire of your mother or your sister or your wife, or any other lady that your fancy dictates. They know. I am sure I don't.

And after it all—

"Oh, dear, dear!" said Margaret; "I *do* wish he didn't have such nice eyes!"

Chapter 6

On the way to luncheon Mr. Woods came upon Adèle Haggage and Hugh Van Orden, both of whom he knew, very much engrossed in one another, in a nook under the stairway. To Billy it seemed just now quite proper that every one should be in love; wasn't it—after all—the most pleasant condition in the world? So he greeted them with a semi-paternal smile that caused Adèle to flush a little.

For she was—let us say, interested—in Mr. Van Orden. That was tolerably well known. In fact, Margaret—prompted by Mrs. Haggage, it must be confessed—had invited him to Selwoode for the especial purpose of entertaining Miss Adèle Haggage; for he was a good match, and Mrs. Haggage, as an experienced chaperon, knew the value of country houses. Very unexpectedly, however, the boy had developed a disconcerting tendency to fall in love with Margaret, who snubbed him promptly and unmercifully. He had accordingly fallen back on Adèle, and Mrs. Haggage had regained both her trust in Providence and her temper.

In the breakfast-room, where luncheon was laid out, the Colonel greeted Mr. Woods with the enthusiasm a sailor shipwrecked on a desert island might conceivably display toward the boat-crew come to rescue him. The Colonel liked Billy; and furthermore, the poor Colonel's position at Selwoode just now was not utterly unlike that of the suppositious mariner; were I minded to venture into metaphor, I should picture him as clinging desperately to the rock of an old fogeyism and surrounded by weltering seas of advanced thought. Colonel Hugonin himself was not advanced in his ideas. Also, he had forceful opinions as to the ultimate destination of those who were.

Then Billy was presented to the men of the party—Mr. Felix Kennaston and Mr. Petheridge Jukesbury. Mrs. Haggage he knew slightly; and Kathleen Saumarez he had known very well indeed, some six years previously, before she had ever heard of Miguel Saumarez, and when Billy was still an undergraduate. She was a widow now, and not well-to-do; and Mr. Woods's first thought on seeing her was that a man was a fool to write verses, and that she looked like just the sort of woman to preserve them.

His second was that he had verged on imbecility when he fancied he admired that slender, dark-haired type. A woman's hair ought to be an enormous coronal of sunlight; a woman ought to have very large, candid eyes of a colour between that of sapphires and that of the spring heavens, only infinitely more beautiful than either; and all petticoated persons differing from this description were manifestly quite unworthy of any serious consideration.

So his eyes turned to Margaret, who had no eyes for him. She had forgotten his existence, with an utterness that verged on ostentation; and if it had been any one else Billy would have surmised she was in a temper. But that angel in a temper!—nonsense! And, oh, what eyes she had! and what lashes! and what hair!—and altogether, how adorable she was, and what a wonder the admiring gods hadn't snatched her up to Olympus long ago!

Thus far Mr. Woods.

But if Miss Hugonin was somewhat taciturn, her counsellors in divers schemes for benefiting the universe were in opulent vein. Billy heard them silently.

"I have spent the entire morning by the lake," Mr. Kennaston informed the party at large, "in company with a mocking-bird who was practising a new aria. It was a wonderful place; the trees were lisping verses to themselves, and the sky overhead was like a robin's egg in colour, and a faint wind was making tucks and ruches and pleats all over the water, quite as if the breezes had set up in business as mantua-makers. I fancy they thought they were working on a great sheet of blue silk, for it was very like that. And every once in a while a fish would leap and leave a splurge of bubble and foam behind that you would have sworn was an inserted lace medallion."

Mr. Kennaston, as you are doubtless aware, is the author of "The King's Quest" and other volumes of verse. He is a full-bodied young man, with hair of no particular shade; and if his green eyes are a little aged, his manner is very youthful. His voice in speaking is wonderfully pleasing, and he has a habit of cocking his head on one side, in a bird-like fashion.

"Indeed," Mr. Petheridge Jukesbury observed, "it is very true that God made the country and man made the town. A little more wine, please."

Mr. Jukesbury is a prominent worker in the cause of philanthropy and temperance. He is ponderous and bland; and for the rest, he is president of the Society for the Suppression of Nicotine and the Nude, vice-president of the Anti-Inebriation League, secretary of the Incorporated Brotherhood of Benevolence, and the bearer of divers similar honours.

"I am never really happy in the country," Mrs. Saumarez dissented;

"it reminds me so constantly of our rural drama. I am always afraid the quartette may come on and sing something."

Kathleen Eppes Saumarez, as I hope you do not need to be told, is the well-known lecturer before women's clubs, and the author of many sympathetic stories of Nature and animal life of the kind that have had such a vogue of late. There was always an indefinable air of pathos about her; as Hunston Wyke put it, one felt, somehow, that her mother had been of a domineering disposition, and that she took after her father.

"Ah, dear lady," Mr. Kennaston cried, playfully, "you, like many of us, have become an alien to Nature in your quest of a mere Earthly Paradox. Epigrams are all very well, but I fancy there is more happiness to be derived from a single impulse from a vernal wood than from a whole problem-play of smart sayings. So few of us are natural," Mr. Kennaston complained, with a dulcet sigh; "we are too sophisticated. Our very speech lacks the tang of outdoor life. Why should we not love Nature— the great mother, who is, I grant you, the necessity of various useful inventions, in her angry moods, but who, in her kindly moments—" He paused, with a wry face. "I beg your pardon," said he, "but I believe I've caught rheumatism lying by that confounded pond."

Mrs. Saumarez rallied the poet, with a pale smile. "That comes of communing with Nature," she reminded him; "and it serves you rightly, for natural communications corrupt good epigrams. I prefer Nature with wide margins and uncut leaves," she spoke, in her best platform manner. "Art should be an expurgated edition of Nature, with all the unpleasant parts left out. And I am sure," Mrs. Saumarez added, handsomely, and clinching her argument, "that Mr. Kennaston gives us much better sunsets in his poems than I have ever seen in the west."

He acknowledged this with a bow.

"Not sherry—claret, if you please," said Mr. Jukesbury. "Art should be an expurgated edition of Nature," he repeated, with a suave chuckle. "Do you know, I consider that admirably put, Mrs. Saumarez—admirably, upon my word. Ah, if our latter-day writers would only take that saying to heart! We do not need to be told of the vice and corruption prevalent, I am sorry to say, among the very best people; what we really need is continually to be reminded of the fact that pure hearts and homes and happy faces are to be found to-day alike in the palatial residences of the wealthy and in the humbler homes of those less abundantly favoured by Fortune, and yet dwelling together in harmony and Christian resignation and—er—comparatively moderate circumstances."

"Surely," Mrs. Saumarez protested, "art has nothing to do with morality. Art is a process. You see a thing in a certain way; you make your reader see it in the same way—or try to. If you succeed, the result is art. If you fail, it may be the book of the year."

"Enduring immortality and—ah—the patronage of the reading public," Mr. Jukesbury placidly insisted, "will be awarded, in the end, only to those who dwell upon the true, the beautiful, and the—er—respectable. Art must cheer; it must be optimistic and edifying and—ah—suitable for young persons; it must have an uplift, a leaven of righteousness, a—er—a sort of moral baking-powder. It must utterly eschew the—ah—unpleasant and repugnant details of life. It is, if I may so express myself, not at home in the ménage à trois or—er—the representation of the nude. Yes, another glass of claret, if you please."

"I quite agree with you," said Mrs. Haggage, in her deep voice. Sarah Ellen Haggage is, of course, the well-known author of "Child-Labour in the South," and "The Down-Trodden Afro-American," and other notable contributions to literature. She is, also, the "Madame President" both of the Society for the Betterment of Civic Government and Sewerage, and of the Ladies' League for the Edification of the Impecunious.

"And I am glad to see," Mrs. Haggage presently went on, "that the literature of the day is so largely beginning to chronicle the sayings and doings of the labouring classes. The virtues of the humble must be admitted in spite of their dissolute and unhygienic tendencies. Yes," Mrs. Haggage added, meditatively, "our literature is undoubtedly acquiring a more elevated tone; at last we are shaking off the scintillant and unwholesome influence of the French."

"Ah, the French!" sighed Mr. Kennaston; "a people who think depravity the soul of wit! Their art is mere artfulness. They care nothing for Nature."

"No," Mrs. Haggage assented; "they prefer nastiness. *All* French books are immoral. I ran across one the other day that was simply hideously indecent—unfit for a modest woman to read. And I can assure you that none of its author's other books are any better. I purchased the entire set at once and read them carefully, in order to make sure that I was perfectly justified in warning my working-girls' classes against them. I wish to misjudge no man—not even a member of a nation notoriously devoted to absinthe and illicit relations."

She breathed heavily, and looked at Mr. Woods as if, somehow, he was responsible. Then she gave the name of the book to Petheridge

Jukesbury. He wished to have it placed on the *Index Expurgatorius* of the Brotherhood of Benevolence, he said.

"Dear, dear," Felix Kennaston sighed, as Mr. Jukesbury made a note of it; "you are all so practical. You perceive an evil and proceed at once, in your common-sense way, to crush it, to stamp it out. Now, I can merely lament certain unfortunate tendencies of the age; I am quite unable to contend against them. Do you know," Mr. Kenneston continued gaily, as he trifled with a bunch of grapes, "I feel horribly out-of-place among you? Here is Mrs. Saumarez creating an epidemic of useful and improving knowledge throughout the country, by means of her charming lectures. Here is Mrs. Haggage, the mainspring, if I may say so, of any number of educational and philanthropic alarm clocks which will some day rouse the sleeping public from its lethargy. And here is my friend Jukesbury, whose eloquent pleas for a higher life have turned so many workmen from gin and improvidence, and which in a printed form are disseminated even in such remote regions as Africa, where I am told they have produced the most satisfactory results upon the unsophisticated but polygamous monarchs of that continent. And here, above all, is Miss Hugonin, utilising the vast power of money—which I am credibly informed is a very good thing to have, though I cannot pretend to speak from experience—and casting whole bakeryfuls of bread upon the waters of charity. And here am I, the idle singer of an empty day—a mere drone in this hive of philanthropic bees! Dear, dear," said Mr. Kennaston, enviously, "what a thing it is to be practical!" And he laughed toward Margaret, in his whimsical way.

Miss Hugonin had been strangely silent; but she returned Mr. Kennaston's smile, and began to take part in the conversation.

"You're only an ignorant child," she rebuked him, "and a very naughty child, too, to make fun of us in this fashion."

"Yes," Mr. Kennaston assented, "I am wilfully ignorant. The world adores ignorance; and where ignorance is kissed it is folly to be wise. To-morrow I shall read you a chapter from my 'Defense of Ignorance,' which my confiding publisher is going to bring out in the autumn."

So the table-talk went on, and now Margaret bore a part therein.

However, I do not think we need record it further.

Mr. Woods listened in a sort of a daze. Adèle Haggage and Hugh Van Orden were conversing in low tones at one end of the table; the Colonel was eating his luncheon, silently and with a certain air of resignation; and so Billy Woods was left alone to attend and marvel.

The ideas they advanced seemed to him, for the most part, sensible. What puzzled him was the uniform gravity which they accorded equally—as it appeared to him—to the discussion of the most pompous platitudes and of the most arrant nonsense. They were always serious; and the general tone of infallibility, Billy thought, could be warranted only by a vast fund of inexperience.

But, in the main, they advocated theories he had always held—excellent theories, he considered. And he was seized with an unreasonable desire to repudiate every one of them.

For it seemed to him that every one of them was aimed at Margaret's approval. It did not matter to whom a remark was ostensibly addressed—always at its conclusion the speaker glanced more or less openly toward Miss Hugonin. She was the audience to which they zealously played, thought Billy; and he wondered.

I think I have said that, owing to the smallness of the house-party, luncheon was served in the breakfast-room. The dining-room at Selwoode is very rarely used, because Margaret declares its size makes a meal there equivalent to eating out-of-doors.

And I must confess that the breakfast-room is far cosier. The room, in the first place, is of reasonable dimensions; it is hung with Flemish tapestries from designs by Van Eyck representing the Four Seasons, but the walls and ceiling are panelled in oak, and over the mantel carved in bas-relief the inevitable Eagle is displayed.

The mantel stood behind Margaret's chair; and over her golden head, half-protectingly, half-threateningly, with his wings outstretched to the uttermost, the Eagle brooded as he had once brooded over Frederick R. Woods. The old man sat contentedly beneath that symbol of what he had achieved in life. He had started (as the phrase runs) from nothing; he had made himself a power. To him, the Eagle meant that crude, incalculable power of wealth he gloried in. And to Billy Woods, the Eagle meant identically the same thing, and—I am sorry to say—he began to suspect that the Eagle was really the audience to whom Miss Hugonin's friends so zealously played.

Perhaps the misanthropy of Mr. Woods was not wholly unconnected with the fact that Margaret never looked at him. *She'd* show him!—the fortune-hunter!

So her eyes never strayed toward him; and her attention never left him. At the end of luncheon she could have enumerated for you every morsel he had eaten, every glare he had directed toward Kennaston, every

　　　　　　　　　　　　　JAMES BRANCH CABELL

beseeching look he had turned to her. Of course, he had taken sherry—dry sherry. Hadn't he told her four years ago—it was the first day she had ever worn the white organdie dotted with purple sprigs, and they sat by the lake so late that afternoon that Frederick R. Woods finally sent for them to come to dinner—hadn't he told her then that only women and children cared for sweet wines? Of course he had—the villain!

Billy, too, had his emotions. To hear that paragon, that queen among women, descant of work done in the slums and of the mysteries of sweat-shops; to hear her state off-hand that there were seventeen hundred and fifty thousand children between the ages of ten and fifteen years employed in the mines and factories of the United States; to hear her discourse of foreign missions as glibly as though she had been born and nurtured in Zambesi Land: all these things filled him with an odd sense of alienation. He wasn't worthy of her, and that was a fact. He was only a dumb idiot, and half the words that were falling thick and fast from philanthropic lips about him might as well have been hailstones, for all the benefit he was deriving from them. He couldn't understand half she said.

In consequence, he very cordially detested the people who could—especially that grimacing ass, Kennaston.

Altogether, neither Mr. Woods nor Miss Hugonin got much comfort from their luncheon.

Chapter 7

After luncheon Billy had a quiet half-hour with the Colonel in the smoking-room.

Said Billy, between puffs of a cigar:

"Peggy's changed a bit."

The Colonel grunted. Perhaps he dared not trust to words.

"Seems to have made some new friends."

A more vigorous grunt.

"Cultured lot, they seem?" said Mr. Woods. "Anxious to do good in the world, too—philanthropic set, eh?"

A snort this time.

"Eh?" said Mr. Woods. There was dawning suspicion in his tone.

The Colonel looked about him. "My boy," said he, "you thank your stars you didn't get that money; and, depend upon it, there never was a gold-ship yet that wasn't followed."

"Pirates?" Billy Woods suggested, helpfully.

"Pirates are human beings," said Colonel Hugonin, with dignity. "Sharks, my boy; sharks!"

Chapter 8

That evening, after proper deliberation, "Célestine," Miss Hugonin commanded, "get out that little yellow dress with the little red bandanna handkerchiefs on it; and for heaven's sake, stop pulling my hair out by the roots, unless you want a *raving* maniac on your hands, Célestine!"

Whereby she had landed me in a quandary. For how, pray, is it possible for me, a simple-minded male, fittingly to depict for you the clothes of Margaret?—the innumerable vanities, the quaint devices, the pleasing conceits with which she delighted to enhance her comeliness? The thing is beyond me. Let us keep discreetly out of her wardrobe, you and I.

Otherwise, I should have to prattle of an infinity of mysteries—of her scarfs, feathers, laces, gloves, girdles, knots, hats, shoes, fans, and slippers—of her embroideries, rings, pins, pendants, ribbons, spangles, bracelets, and chains—in fine, there would be no end to the list of gewgaws that went to make Margaret Hugonin even more adorable than Nature had fashioned her. For when you come to think of it, it takes the craft and skill and life-work of a thousand men to dress one girl properly; and in Margaret's case, I protest that every one of them, could he have beheld the result of their united labours, would have so gloried in his own part therein that there would have been no putting up with any of the lot.

Yet when I think of the tiny shoes she affected—patent-leather ones mostly, with a seam running straight up the middle (and you may guess the exact date of our comedy by knowing in what year these shoes were modish); the string of fat pearls she so often wore about her round, full throat; the white frock, say, with arabesques of blue all over it, that Felix Kennaston said reminded him of Ruskin's tombstone; or that other white-and-blue one—*décolleté*, that was—which I swear seraphic mantua-makers had woven out of mists and the skies of June: when I remember these things, I repeat, almost am I tempted to become a boot-maker and a lapidary and a milliner and, in fine, an adept in all the other arts and trades and sciences that go to make a well-groomed American girl what she is—the incredible fruit of grafted centuries, the period after the list of Time's achievements—just that I might describe Margaret to you properly.

But the thing is beyond me. I leave such considerations, then, to Célestine, and resolve for the future rigorously to eschew all such gauds. Meanwhile, if an untutored masculine description will content you—

Margaret, I have on reliable feminine authority, was one of the very few blondes whose complexions can carry off reds and yellows. This particular gown—I remember it perfectly—was of a dim, dull yellow—flounciful (if I may coin a word), diaphanous, expansive. I have not the least notion what fabric composed it; but scattered about it, in unexpected places, were diamond-shaped red things that I am credibly informed are called medallions. The general effect of it may be briefly characterised as grateful to the eye and dangerous to the heart, and to a rational train of thought quite fatal.

For it was cut low in the neck; and Margaret's neck and shoulders would have drawn madrigals from a bench of bishops.

And in consequence, Billy Woods ate absolutely no dinner that evening.

Chapter 9

It was an hour or two later when the moon, drifting tardily up from the south, found Miss Hugonin and Mr. Kennaston chatting amicably together in the court at Selwoode. They were discussing the deplorable tendencies of the modern drama.

The court at Selwoode lies in the angle of the building, the ground plan of which is L-shaped. Its two outer sides are formed by covered cloisters leading to the palm-garden, and by moonlight—the night bland and sweet with the odour of growing things, vocal with plashing fountains, spangled with fire-flies that flicker indolently among a glimmering concourse of nymphs and fauns eternally postured in flight or in pursuit—by moonlight, I say, the court at Selwoode is perhaps as satisfactory a spot for a *tête-à-tête* as this transitory world affords.

Mr. Kennaston was in vein to-night; he scintillated; he was also a little nervous. This was probably owing to the fact that Margaret, leaning against the back of the stone bench on which they both sat, her chin propped by her hand, was gazing at him in that peculiar, intent fashion of hers which—as I think I have mentioned—caused you fatuously to believe she had forgotten there were any other trousered beings extant.

Mr. Kennaston, however, stuck to apt phrases and nice distinctions. The moon found it edifying, but rather dull.

After a little Mr. Kennaston paused in his boyish, ebullient speech, and they sat in silence. The lisping of the fountains was very audible. In the heavens, the moon climbed a little further and registered a manifestly impossible hour on the sun-dial. It also brightened.

It was a companionable sort of a moon. It invited talk of a confidential nature.

"Bless my soul," it was signalling to any number of gentlemen at that moment, "there's only you and I and the girl here. Speak out, man! She'll have you now, if she ever will. You'll never have a chance like this again, I can tell you. Come, now, my dear boy, I'm shining full in your face, and you've no idea how becoming it is. I'm not like that garish, blundering sun, who doesn't know any better than to let her see how red and fidgetty you get when you're excited; I'm an old hand at such matters. I've presided over these little affairs since Babylon was a paltry village. *I'll* never tell. And—and if anything should happen, I'm always ready to go behind a cloud, you know. So, speak out!—speak out, man, if you've the heart of a mouse!"

Thus far the conscienceless spring moon.

Mr. Kennaston sighed. The moon took this as a promising sign and brightened over it perceptibly, and thereby afforded him an excellent gambit.

"Yes?" said Margaret. "What is it, beautiful?"

That, in privacy, was her fantastic name for him.

The poet laughed a little. "Beautiful child," said he—and that, under similar circumstances, was his perfectly reasonable name for her—"I have been discourteous. To be frank, I have been sulking as irrationally as a baby who clamours for the moon yonder."

"You aren't really anything but a baby, you know." Indeed, Margaret almost thought of him as such. He was so delightfully naïf.

He bent toward her. A faint tremor woke in his speech. "And so," said he, softly, "I cry for the moon—the unattainable, exquisite moon. It is very ridiculous, is it not?"

But he did not look at the moon. He looked toward Margaret—past Margaret, toward the gleaming windows of Selwoode, where the Eagle brooded:

"Oh, I really can't say," Margaret cried, in haste. "She was kind to Endymion, you know. We will hope for the best. I think we'd better go into the house now."

"You bid me hope?" said he.

"Beautiful, if you really want the moon, I don't see the *least* objection to your continuing to hope. They make so many little airships and things nowadays, you know, and you'll probably find it only green cheese, after all. What *is* green cheese, I wonder?—it sounds horribly indigestible and unattractive, doesn't it?" Miss Hugonin babbled, in a tumult of fear and disappointment. He was about to spoil their friendship now; men were so utterly inconsiderate. "I'm a little cold," said she, mendaciously, "I really must go in."

He detained her. "Surely," he breathed, "you must know what I have so long wanted to tell you—"

"I haven't the *least* idea," she protested, promptly. "You can tell me all about it in the morning. I have some accounts to cast up to-night. Besides, I'm not a good person to tell secrets to. You—you'd much better not tell me. Oh, really, Mr. Kennaston," she cried, earnestly, "you'd much better not tell me!"

"Ah, Margaret, Margaret," he pleaded, "I am not adamant. I am only a man, with a man's heart that hungers for you, cries for you, clamours for you day by day! I love you, beautiful child—love you with a poet's love that is alien to these sordid days, with a love that is half worship. I love you as Leander loved his Hero, as Pyramus loved Thisbe. Ah, child, child, how beautiful you are! You are fairest of created women, child—fair as those long-dead queens for whose smiles old cities burned and kingdoms were lightly lost. I am mad for love of you! Ah, have pity upon me, Margaret, for I love you very tenderly!"

He delivered these observations with appropriate fervour.

"Mr. Kennaston," said she, "I am sorry. We got along so nicely before, and I was *so* proud of your friendship. We've had such good times together, you and I, and I've liked your verses so, and I've liked you—Oh, please, *please*, let's keep on being just friends!" Margaret wailed, piteously.

"Friends!" he cried, and gave a bitter laugh. "I was never friends with you, Margaret. Why, even as I read my verses to you—those pallid, ineffectual verses that praised you timorously under varied names—even then there pulsed in my veins the riotous pæan of love, the great mad song of love that shamed my paltry rhymes. I cannot be friends with you, child! I must have all or nothing. Bid me hope or go!"

Miss Hugonin meditated for a moment and did neither.

"Beautiful," she presently queried, "would you be very, very much shocked if I descended to slang?"

"I think," said he, with an uncertain smile, "that I could endure it."

"Why, then—cut it out, beautiful! Cut it out! I don't believe a word you've said, in the first place; and, anyhow, it annoys me to have you talk to me like that. I don't like it, and it simply makes me awfully, awfully tired."

With which characteristic speech, Miss Hugonin leaned back and sat up very rigidly and smiled at him like a cherub.

Kennaston groaned.

"It shall be as you will," he assured her, with a little quaver in his speech that was decidedly effective. "And in any event, I am not sorry that I have loved you, beautiful child. You have always been a power for good in my life. You have gladdened me with the vision of a beauty that is more than human, you have heartened me for this petty business of living, you have praised my verses, you have even accorded me certain pecuniary assistance as to their publication—though I must admit that to accept it of you was very distasteful to me. Ah!" Felix Kennaston cried, with a quick lift of speech, "impractical child that I am, I had not thought of that! My love had caused me to forget the great barrier that stands between us."

He gasped and took a short turn about the court.

"Pardon me, Miss Hugonin," he entreated, when his emotions were under a little better control, "for having spoken as I did. I had forgotten. Think of me, if you will, as no better than the others—think of me as a mere fortune-hunter. My presumption will be justly punished."

"Oh, no, no, it isn't that," she cried; "it isn't that, is it? You—you would care just as much about me if I were poor, wouldn't you, beautiful? I don't want you to care for me, of course," Margaret added, with haste. "I want to go on being friends. Oh, that money, that *nasty* money!" she cried, in a sudden gust of petulance. "It makes me so distrustful, and I can't help it!"

He smiled at her wistfully. "My dear," said he, "are there no mirrors at Selwoode to remove your doubts?"

"I—yes, I do believe in you," she said, at length. "But I don't want to marry you. You see, I'm not a bit in love with you," Margaret explained, candidly.

Ensued a silence. Mr. Kennaston bowed his head.

"You bid me go?" said he.

"No—not exactly," said she.

He indicated a movement toward her.

"Now, you needn't attempt to take any liberties with me," Miss Hugonin announced, decisively, "because if you do I'll never speak to you again. You must let me go now. You—you must let me think."

Then Felix Kennaston acted very wisely. He rose and stood aside, with a little bow.

"I can wait, child," he said, sadly. "I have already waited a long time."

Miss Hugonin escaped into the house without further delay. It was very flattering, of course; he had spoken beautifully, she thought, and nobly and poetically and considerately, and altogether there was absolutely no excuse for her being in a temper. Still, she was.

The moon, however, considered the affair as arranged.

For she had been no whit more resolute in her refusal, you see, than becomes any self-respecting maid. In fact, she had not refused him; and the experienced moon had seen the hopes of many a wooer thrive, chameleon-like, on answers far less encouraging than that which Margaret had given Felix Kennaston.

Margaret was very fond of him. All women like a man who can do a picturesque thing without bothering to consider whether or not he be making himself ridiculous; and more than once in thinking of him she had wondered if—perhaps—possibly—some day—? And always these vague flights of fancy had ended at this precise point—incinerated, if you will grant me the simile, by the sudden flaming of her cheeks.

The thing is common enough. You may remember that Romeo was not the only gentleman that Juliet noticed at her début: there was the young Petruchio; and the son and heir of old Tiberio; and I do not question that she had a kind glance or so for County Paris. Beyond doubt, there were many with whom my lady had danced; with whom she had laughed a little; with whom she had exchanged a few perfectly affable words and looks—when of a sudden her heart speaks: "Who's he that would not dance? If he be married, my grave is like to prove my marriage-bed." In any event, Paris and Petruchio and Tiberio's young hopeful can go hang; Romeo has come.

Romeo is seldom the first. Pray you, what was there to prevent Juliet from admiring So-and-so's dancing? or from observing that Signor Such-an-one had remarkably expressive eyes? or from thinking of Tybalt as a dear, reckless fellow whom it was the duty of some good woman to rescue from perdition? If no one blames the young Montague for sending Rosaline to the right-about—Rosaline for whom he was weeping and rhyming an hour before—why, pray, should not Signorina Capulet have had a few previous *affaires du coeur*? Depend upon it, she had; for was she not already past thirteen?

In like manner, I dare say that a deal passed between Desdemona and Cassio that the honest Moor never knew of; and that Lucrece was probably very pleasant and agreeable to Tarquin, as a well-bred hostess should be; and that Helen had that little affair with Theseus before she ever thought of Paris; and that if Cleopatra died for love of Antony it was not until she had previously lived a great while with Cæsar.

So Felix Kennaston had his hour. Now Margaret has gone into Selwoode, flame-faced and quite unconscious that she is humming under her breath the words of a certain inane old song:

> "Oh, she sat for me a chair;
> She has ringlets in her hair;
> She's a young thing and cannot leave her mother"—

Only she sang it "father." And afterward, she suddenly frowned and stamped her foot, did Margaret.

"I *hate* him!" said she; but she looked very guilty.

Chapter 10

In the living-hall of Selwoode Miss Hugonin paused. Undeniably there were the accounts of the Ladies' League for the Edification of the Impecunious to be put in order; her monthly report as treasurer was due in a few days, and Margaret was in such matters a careful, painstaking body, and not wholly dependent upon her secretary; but she was entirely too much out of temper to attend to that now.

It was really all Mr. Kennaston's fault, she assured a pricking conscience, as she went out on the terrace before Selwoode. He had bothered her dreadfully.

There she found Petheridge Jukesbury smoking placidly in the effulgence of the moonlight; and the rotund, pasty countenance he turned toward her was ludicrously like the moon's counterfeit in muddy water. I am sorry to admit it, but Mr. Jukesbury had dined somewhat injudiciously. You are not to stretch the phrase; he was merely prepared to accord the universe his approval, to pat Destiny upon the head, and his thoughts ran clear enough, but with Aprilian counter-changes of the jovial and the lachrymose.

"Ah, Miss Hugonin," he greeted her, with a genial smile, "I am indeed fortunate. You find me deep in meditation, and also, I am sorry to say, in the practise of a most pernicious habit. You do not object? Ah, that is so like you. You are always kind, Miss Hugonin. Your kindness, which falls, if I may so express myself, as the gentle rain from Heaven upon all deserving charitable institutions, and daily comforts the destitute with good advice and consoles the sorrowing with blankets, would now induce you to tolerate an odour which I am sure is personally distasteful to you."

"But *really* I don't mind," was Margaret's protest.

"I cannot permit it," Mr. Jukesbury insisted, and waved a pudgy hand in the moonlight. "No, really, I cannot permit it. We will throw it away, if you please, and say no more about it," and his glance followed the glowing flight of his cigar-end somewhat wistfully. "Your father's cigars are such as it is seldom my privilege to encounter; but, then, my personal habits are not luxurious, nor my private income precisely what my childish imaginings had pictured it at this comparatively advanced period of life. Ah, youth, youth!—as the poet admirably says, Miss Hugonin, the thoughts of youth are long, long thoughts, but its visions of existence are rose-tinged and free from care, and its conception of the responsibilities of manhood—such as taxes and the water-rate—I may safely characterise as extremely sketchy. But pray be seated, Miss Hugonin," Petheridge Jukesbury blandly urged.

Common courtesy forced her to comply. So Margaret seated herself on a little red rustic bench. In the moonlight—but I think I have mentioned how Margaret looked in the moonlight; and above her golden head the Eagle, sculptured over the door-way, stretched his wings to the uttermost, half-protectingly, half-threateningly, and seemed to view Mr. Jukesbury with a certain air of expectation.

"A beautiful evening," Petheridge Jukesbury suggested, after a little cogitation.

She conceded that this was undeniable.

"Where Nature smiles, and only the conduct of man is vile and altogether what it ought not to be," he continued, with unction—"ah, how true that is and how consoling! It is a good thing to meditate upon our own vileness, Miss Hugonin—to reflect that we are but worms with naturally the most vicious inclinations. It is most salutary. Even I am but a worm, Miss Hugonin, though the press has been pleased to speak most kindly of me. Even you—ah, no!" cried Mr. Jukesbury, kissing his finger-tips, with gallantry; "let us say a worm who has burst its cocoon and become a butterfly—a butterfly with a charming face and a most charitable disposition and considerable property!"

Margaret thanked him with a smile, and began to think wistfully of the Ladies' League accounts. Still, he was a good man; and she endeavoured to persuade herself that she considered his goodness to atone for his flabbiness and his fleshiness and his interminable verbosity—which she didn't.

Mr. Jukesbury sighed.

"A naughty world," said he, with pathos—"a very naughty world, which really does not deserve the honour of including you in its census reports. Yet I dare say it has the effrontery to put you down in the tax-lists; it even puts me down—me, an humble worker in the vineyard, with both hands set to the plough. And if I don't pay up it sells me out. A very naughty world, indeed! I dare say," Mr. Jukesbury observed, raising his eyes—not toward heaven, but toward the Eagle, "that its conduct, as the poet says, creates considerable distress among the angels. I don't know. I am not acquainted with many angels. My wife was an angel, but she is now a lifeless form. She has been for five years.

I erected a tomb to her at considerable personal expense, but I don't begrudge it—no, I don't begrudge it, Miss Hugonin. She was very hard to live with. But she was an angel, and angels are rare. Miss Hugonin," said Petheridge Jukesbury, with emphasis, "*you* are an angel."

"Oh, dear, *dear!*" said Margaret, to herself; "I do wish I'd gone to bed directly after dinner!"

Above them the Eagle brooded.

"Surely," he breathed, "you must know what I have so long wanted to tell you—"

"No," said Margaret, "and I don't want to know, please. You make me awfully tired, and I don't care for you in the *least*. Now, you let go my hand—let go at once!"

He detained her. "You are an angel," he insisted—"an angel with a large property. I love you, Margaret! Be mine!—be my blushing bride, I entreat you! Your property is far too large for an angel to look after. You need a man of affairs. I am a man of affairs. I am forty-five, and have no bad habits. My press-notices are, as a rule, favourable, my eloquence is accounted considerable, and my dearest aspiration is that you will comfort my declining years. I might add that I adore you, but I think I mentioned that before. Margaret, will you be my blushing bride?"

"No!" said Miss Hugonin emphatically. "No, you tipsy old beast—no!"

There was a rustle of skirts. The door slammed, and the philanthropist was left alone on the terrace.

Chapter 11

I n the living-hall Margaret came upon Hugh Van Orden, who was searching in one of the alcoves for a piece of music that Adèle Haggage wanted and had misplaced.

The boy greeted her miserably.

"Miss Hugonin," he lamented, "you're awfully hard on me."

"I am sorry," said Margaret, "that you consider me discourteous to a guest in my own house." Oh, I grant you Margaret was in a temper now.

"It isn't that," he protested; "but I never see you alone. And I've had something to tell you."

"Yes?" said she, coldly.

He drew near to her. "Surely," he breathed, "you must know what I have long wanted to tell you—"

"Yes, I should think I *did!*" said Margaret, "and if you dare tell me a word of it I'll never speak to you again. It's getting a little monotonous. Good-night, Mr. Van Orden."

Half way up the stairs she paused and ran lightly back.

"Oh, Hugh, Hugh!" she said, contritely, "I was unpardonably rude. I'm sorry, dear, but it's quite impossible. You are a dear, cute little boy, and I love you—but not that way. So let's shake hands, Hugh, and be friends! And then you can go and play with Adèle." He raised her hand to his lips. He really was a nice boy.

"But, oh, dear!" said Margaret, when he had gone; "what horrid creatures men are, and what a temper I'm in, and what a vexatious place the world is! I wish I were a pauper! I wish I had never been born! And I wish—and I wish I had those League papers fixed! I'll do it to-night! I'm sure I need something tranquillising, like assessments and decimal places and unpaid dues, to keep me from *screaming*. I hate them all—all three of them—as badly as I do *him!*"

Thereupon she blushed, for no apparent reason, and went to her own rooms in a frame of mind that was inexcusable, but very becoming. Her cheeks burned, her eyes flashed with a brighter glow that was gem-like and a little cruel, and her chin tilted up defiantly. Margaret had a resolute chin, a masculine chin. I fancy that it was only at the last moment that Nature found it a thought too boyish and modified it with a dimple—a very creditable dimple, by the way, that she must have been really proud of. That ridiculous little dint saved it, feminised it.

Altogether, then, she swept down upon the papers of the Ladies' League for the Edification of the Impecunious with very much the look of a diminutive Valkyrie—a Valkyrie of unusual personal attractions, you understand—*en route* for the battle-field and a little, a very little eager and expectant of the strife.

Subsequently, "Oh, dear, *dear!*" said she, amid a feverish rustling of papers; "the whole world is out of sorts to-night! I never *did* know how much seven times eight is, and I hate everybody, and I've left that list of unpaid dues in Uncle Fred's room, and I've got to go after it, and I don't want to! Bother those little suitors of mine!"

Miss Hugonin rose, and went out from her own rooms, carrying a bunch of keys, across the hallway to the room in which Frederick R. Woods had died. It was his study, you may remember. It had been little used since his death, but Margaret kept her less important papers there—the overflow, the flotsam of her vast philanthropic and educational correspondence.

And there she found Billy Woods.

Chapter 12

His back was turned to the door as she entered. He was staring at a picture beside the mantel—a portrait of Frederick R. Woods—and his eyes when he wheeled about were wistful.

Then, on a sudden, they lighted up as if they had caught fire from hers, and his adoration flaunted crimson banners in his cheeks, and his heart, I dare say, was a great blaze of happiness. He loved her, you see; when she entered a room it really made a difference to this absurd young man. He saw a great many lights, for instance, and heard music. And accordingly, he laughed now in a very contented fashion.

"I wasn't burglarising," said he—"that is, not exactly. I ought to have asked your permission, I suppose, before coming here, but I couldn't find you, and—and it was rather important. You see," Mr. Woods continued, pointing to the great carved desk. "I happened to speak of this desk to the Colonel to-night. We—we were talking of Uncle Fred's death, and I found out, quite by accident, that it hadn't been searched since then—that is, not thoroughly. There are secret drawers, you see; one here," and he touched the spring that threw it open, "and the other on this side. There is—there is nothing of importance in them; only receipted bills and such. The other drawer is inside that centre compartment, which is locked. The Colonel wouldn't come. He said it was all foolishness, and that he had a book he wanted to read. So he sent me after what he called my mare's nest. It isn't, you see—no, not quite, not quite," Mr. Woods murmured, with an odd smile, and then laughed and added, lamely: "I—I suppose I'm the only person who knew about it."

Mr. Woods's manner was a thought strange. He stammered a little in speaking; he laughed unnecessarily; and Margaret could see that his hands trembled. Taking him all in all, you would have sworn he was repressing some vital emotion. But he did not seem unhappy—no, not exactly unhappy. He was with Margaret, you see.

"Oh, you beauty!" his meditations ran.

He had some excuse. In the soft, rosy twilight of the room—the study at Selwoode is panelled in very dark oak, and the doors and windows are screened with crimson hangings—her parti-coloured red-and-yellow gown might have been a scrap of afterglow left over from an unusually fine sunset. In a word, Miss Hugonin was a very quaint and colourful and delectable figure as she came a little further into the room. Her eyes shone like blue stars, and her hair shone—there must be pounds of it, Billy thought—and her very shoulders, plump, flawless, ineffable, shone with the glow of an errant cloud-tatter that is just past the track of dawn, and is therefore neither pink nor white, but manages somehow to combine the best points of both colours.

"Ah, indeed?" said Miss Hugonin. Her tone imparted a surprising degree of chilliness to this simple remark.

"No," she went on, very formally, "this is not a private room; you owe me no apology for being here. Indeed, I am rather obliged to you, Mr. Woods, for none of us knew of these secret drawers. Here is the key to the central compartment, if you will be kind enough to point out the other one. Dear, dear!" Margaret concluded, languidly, "all this is quite like a third-rate melodrama. I haven't the least doubt you will discover a will in there in your favour, and be reinstated as the long-lost heir and all that sort of thing. How tiresome that will be for me, though."

She was in a mood to be cruel to-night. She held out the keys to him, in a disinterested fashion, and dropped them daintily into his outstretched palm, just as she might have given a coin to an unusually grimy mendicant. But the tips of her fingers grazed his hand.

That did the mischief. Her least touch was enough to set every nerve in his body a-tingle. "Peggy!" he said hoarsely, as the keys jangled to the floor. Then Mr. Woods drew a little nearer to her and said "Peggy, Peggy!" in a voice that trembled curiously, and appeared to have no intention of saying anything further.

Indeed, words would have seemed mere tautology to any one who could have seen his eyes. Margaret looked into them for a minute, and her own eyes fell before their blaze, and her heart—very foolishly—stood still for a breathing-space. Subsequently she recalled the fact that he was a fortune-hunter, and that she despised him, and also observed—to her surprise and indignation—that he was holding her hand and had apparently been doing so for some time. You may believe it, that she withdrew that pink-and-white trifle angrily enough.

"Pray don't be absurd, Mr. Woods," said she.

Billy caught up the word. "Absurd!" he echoed—"yes, that describes what I've been pretty well, doesn't it, Peggy? I *was* absurd when I let you send me to the right-about four years ago. I realised that to-day the moment I saw you. I should have held on like the very grimmest death; I should have bullied you into marrying me, if necessary, and in spite of fifty Anstruthers. Oh, yes, I know that now. But I was only a boy then, Peggy, and so I let a boy's pride come between us. I know now there isn't any question of pride where you are concerned—not any question of pride nor of any silly misunderstandings, nor of any uncle's wishes, nor of anything but just you, Peggy. It's just you that I care for now—just you."

"Ah!" Margaret cried, with a swift intake of the breath that was almost a sob. He had dared, after all; oh, it was shameless, sordid! And yet (she thought dimly), how dear that little quiver in his voice had been were it unplanned!—and how she could have loved this big, eager boy were he not the hypocrite she knew him!

She'd show him! But somehow—though it was manifestly what he deserved—she found she couldn't look him in the face while she did it.

So she dropped her eyes to the floor and waited for a moment of tense silence. Then, "Am I to consider this a proposal, Mr. Woods?" she asked, in muffled tones.

Billy stared. "Yes," said he, very gravely, after an interval.

"You see," she explained, still in the same dull voice, "you phrased it so vaguely I couldn't well be certain. You don't propose very well, Mr. Woods. I—I've had opportunities to become an authority on such matters, you see, since I've been rich. That makes a difference, doesn't it? A great many men are willing to marry me now who wouldn't have thought of such a thing, say—say, four years ago. So I've had some experience. Oh, yes, three—three *persons* have offered to marry me for my money earlier in this very evening—before you did, Mr. Woods. And, really, I can't compliment you on your methods, Mr. Woods; they are a little vague, a little abrupt, a little transparent, don't you think?"

"Peggy!" he cried, in a frightened whisper. He could not believe, you see, that it was the woman he loved who was speaking.

And for my part, I admit frankly that at this very point, if ever in her life, Margaret deserved a thorough shaking.

"Dear me," she airily observed, "I'm sure I've said nothing out of the way. I think it speaks very well for you that you're so fond of your old home—so anxious to regain it at *any* cost. It's quite touching, Mr. Woods."

She raised her eyes toward his. I dare say she was suffering as much as he. But women consider it a point of honour to smile when they stab; Margaret smiled with an innocence that would have seemed overdone in an angel.

Then, in an instant, she had the grace to be abjectly ashamed of herself. Billy's face had gone white. His mouth was set, mask-like, and his breathing was a little perfunctory. It stung her, though, that he was not angry. He was sorry.

"I—I see," he said, very carefully. "You think I—want the money. Yes—I see."

"And why not?" she queried, pleasantly. "Dear me, money's a very sensible thing to want, I'm sure. It makes a great difference, you know."

He looked down into her face for a moment. One might have sworn this detected fortune-hunter pitied her.

"Yes," he assented, slowly, "it makes a difference—not a difference for the better, I'm afraid, Peggy."

Ensued a silence.

Then Margaret tossed her head. She was fast losing her composure. She would have given the world to retract what she had said, and accordingly she resolved to brazen it out.

"You needn't look at me as if I were a convicted criminal," she said, sharply. "I won't marry you, and there's an end of it."

"It isn't that I'm thinking of," said Mr. Woods, with a grave smile. "You see, it takes me a little time to realise your honest opinion of me. I believe I understand now. You think me a very hopeless cad—that's about your real opinion, isn't it, Peggy? I didn't know that, you see. I thought you knew me better than that. You did once, Peggy—once, a long time ago, and—and I hoped you hadn't quite forgotten that time."

The allusion was ill chosen.

"Oh, oh, *oh!* " she cried, gasping. "*You* to remind me of that time!— you of all men. Haven't you a vestige of shame? Haven't you a rag of honour left? Oh, I didn't know there were such men in the world! And to think—to think—" Margaret's glorious voice broke, and she wrung her hands helplessly.

Then, after a little, she raised her eyes to his, and spoke without a trace of emotion. "To think," she said, and her voice was toneless now, "to think that I loved you! It's that that hurts, you know. For I loved you very dearly, Billy Woods—yes, I think I loved you quite as much as any woman can ever love a man. You were the first, you see, and girls—girls are very foolish about such things. I thought you were brave, and strong, and clean, and honest, and beautiful, and dear—oh, quite the best and dearest man in the world, I thought you, Billy Woods! That—that was queer, wasn't it?" she asked, with a listless little shiver. "Yes, it was very queer. You didn't think of me in quite that way, did you? No, you—you thought I was well enough to amuse you for a while. I was well enough for a summer flirtation, wasn't I, Billy? But marriage—ah, no, you never thought of marriage then. You ran away when Uncle Fred suggested that. You refused point-blank—refused in this very room—didn't you, Billy? Ah, that—that hurt," Margaret ended, with a faint smile. "Yes, it—hurt."

Billy Woods raised a protesting hand, as though to speak, but afterward he drew a deep, tremulous breath and bit his lip and was silent.

She had spoken very quietly, very simply, very like a tired child; now her voice lifted. "But you've hurt me more to-night," she said, equably— "to-night, when you've come cringing back to me—to me, whom you'd have none of when I was poor. I'm rich now, though. That makes a difference, doesn't it, Billy? You're willing to whistle back the girl's love you flung away once—yes, quite willing. But can't you understand how much it must hurt me to think I ever loved you?" Margaret asked, very gently.

She wanted him to understand. She wanted him to be ashamed. She prayed God that he might be just a little, little bit ashamed, so that she might be able to forgive him.

But he stood silent, bending puzzled brows toward her.

"Can't you understand, Billy?" she pleaded, softly. "I can't help seeing what a cur you are. I must hate you, Billy—of course, I must," she insisted, very gently, as though arguing the matter with herself; then suddenly she sobbed and wrung her hands in anguish. "Oh, I can't, I can't!" she wailed. "God help me, I can't hate you, even though I know you for what you are!"

His arms lifted a little; and in a flash Margaret knew that what she most wanted in all the world was to have them close about her, and then to lay her head upon his shoulder and cry contentedly.

Oh, she did want to forgive him! If he had lost all sense of shame, why could he not lie to her? Surely, he could at least lie? And, oh, how gladly she would believe!—only the tiniest, the flimsiest fiction, her eyes craved of him.

But he merely said "I see—I see," very slowly, and then smiled. "We'll put the money aside just now," he said. "Perhaps, after a little, we—we'll came back to that. I think you've forgotten, though, that when—when Uncle Fred and I had our difference you had just thrown me over—had just ordered me never to speak to you again? I couldn't very well ask you to marry me, could I, under those circumstances?"

"I spoke in a moment of irritation," a very dignified Margaret pointed out; "you would have paid no attention whatever to it if you had really—cared."

Billy laughed, rather sadly. "Oh, I cared right enough," he said. "I still care. The question is—do you?"

"No," said Margaret, with decision, "I don't—not in the *least*."

"Peggy," Mr. Woods commanded, "look at me!"

"You have had your answer, I think," Miss Hugonin indifferently observed.

Billy caught her chin in his hand and turned her face to his. "Peggy, do you—care?" he asked, softly.

And Margaret looked into his honest-seeming eyes and, in a panic, knew that her traitor lips were forming "yes."

"That would be rather unfortunate, wouldn't it?" she asked, with a smile. "You see, it was only an hour ago I promised to marry Mr. Kennaston."

"Kennaston!" Billy gasped. "You—you don't mean that you care for *him*, Peggy?"

"I really can't see why it should concern you," said Margaret, sweetly, "but since you ask—I do. You couldn't expect me to remain inconsolable forever, you know."

Then the room blurred before her eyes. She stood rigid, defiant. She was dimly aware that Billy was speaking, speaking from a great distance, it seemed, and then after a century or two his face came back to her out of the whirl of things. And, though she did not know it, they were smiling bravely at one another.

"—and so," Mr. Woods was stating, "I've been an even greater ass than usual, and I hope you'll be very, very happy."

"Thank you," she returned, mechanically, "I—I hope so."

After an interval, "Good-night, Peggy," said Mr. Woods.

"Oh—? Good-night," said she, with a start.

He turned to go. Then, "By Jove!" said he, grimly, "I've been so busy making an ass of myself I'd forgotten all about more—more important things."

Mr. Woods picked up the keys and, going to the desk, unlocked the centre compartment with a jerk. Afterward he gave a sharp exclamation. He had found a paper in the secret drawer at the back which appeared to startle him.

Billy unfolded it slowly, with a puzzled look growing in his countenance. Then for a moment Margaret's golden head drew close to his yellow curls and they read it through together. And in the most melodramatic and improbable fashion in the world they found it to be the last will and testament of Frederick R. Woods.

"But—but I don't understand," was Miss Hugonin's awed comment. "It's exactly like the other will, only—why, it's dated the seventeenth of June, the day before he died! And it's witnessed by Hodges and Burton—the butler and the first footman, you know—and they've never said anything about such a paper. And, then, why should he have made another will just like the first?"

Billy pondered.

By and bye, "I think I can explain that," he said, in a rather peculiar voice. "You see, Hodges and Burton witnessed all his papers, half the time without knowing what they were about. They would hardly have thought of this particular one after his death. And it isn't quite the same will as the other; it leaves you practically everything, but it doesn't appoint any trustees, as the other did, because this will was drawn up after you were of age. Moreover, it contains these four bequests to colleges, to establish a Woods chair of ethnology, which the other will didn't provide for. Of course, it would have been simpler merely to add a codicil to the first will, but Uncle Fred was always very methodical. I—I think he was probably going through the desk the night he died, destroying various papers. He must have taken the other will out to destroy it just—just before he died. Perhaps—perhaps—" Billy paused for a little and then laughed, unmirthfully. "It scarcely matters," said he. "Here is the will. It is undoubtedly genuine and undoubtedly the last he made. You'll have to have it probated, Peggy, and settle with the colleges. It—it won't make much of a hole in the Woods millions."

There was a half-humorous bitterness in his voice that Margaret noted silently. So (she thought) he had hoped for a moment that at the last Frederick R. Woods had relented toward him. It grieved her, in a dull fashion, to see him so mercenary. It grieved her—though she would have denied it emphatically—to see him so disappointed. Since he wanted the money so much, she would have liked for him to have had it, worthless as he was, for the sake of the boy he had been.

"Thank you," she said, coldly, as she took the paper; "I will give it to my father. He will do what is necessary. Good-night, Mr. Woods."

Then she locked up the desk in a businesslike fashion and turned to him, and held out her hand.

"Good-night, Billy," said this perfectly inconsistent young woman. "For a moment I thought Uncle Fred had altered his will in your favour. I almost wish he had."

Billy smiled a little.

"That would never have done," he said, gravely, as he shook hands; "you forget what a sordid, and heartless, and generally good-for-nothing chap I am, Peggy. It's much better as it is."

Only the tiniest, the flimsiest fiction, her eyes craved of him. Even now, at the eleventh hour, lie to me, Billy Woods, and, oh, how gladly I will believe!

But he merely said "Good-night, Peggy," and went out of the room. His broad shoulders had a pathetic droop, a listlessness.

Margaret was glad. Of course, she was glad. At last, she had told him exactly what she thought of him. Why shouldn't she be glad? She was delighted.

So, by way of expressing this delight, she sat down at the desk and began to cry very softly.

Chapter 13

Having duly considered the emptiness of existence, the unworthiness of men, the dreary future that awaited her—though this did not trouble her greatly, as she confidently expected to die soon—and many other such dolorous topics, Miss Hugonin decided to retire for the night. She rose, filled with speculations as to the paltriness of life and the probability of her eyes being red in the morning.

"It will be all his fault if they are," she consoled herself. "Doubtless he'll be very much pleased. After robbing me of all faith in humanity, I dare say the one thing needed to complete his happiness is to make me look like a fright. I hate him! After making me miserable, now, I suppose he'll go off and make some other woman miserable. Oh, of course, he'll make love to the first woman he meets who has any money. I'm sure she's welcome to him. I only pity any woman who has to put up with *him*. No, I don't," Margaret decided, after reflection; "I hate her, too!"

Miss Hugonin went to the door leading to the hallway and paused. Then—I grieve to relate it—she shook a little pink-tipped fist in the air.

"I detest you!" she commented, between her teeth; "oh, how *dare* you make me feel so ashamed of the way I've treated you!"

The query—as possibly you may have divined—was addressed to Mr. Woods. He was standing by the fireplace in the hallway, and his tall figure was outlined sharply against the flame of the gas-logs that burned there. His shoulders had a pathetic droop, a listlessness.

Billy was reading a paper of some kind by the firelight, and the black outline of his face smiled grimly over it. Then he laughed and threw it into the fire.

"Billy!" a voice observed—a voice that was honey and gold and velvet and all that is most sweet and rich and soft in the world.

Mr. Woods was aware of a light step, a swishing, sibilant, delightful rustling—the caress of sound is the rustling of a well-groomed woman's skirts—and of an afterthought of violets, of a mere reminiscence of orris, all of which came toward him through the dimness of the hall. He started, noticeably.

"Billy," Miss Hugonin stated, "I'm sorry for what I said to you. I'm not sure it isn't true, you know, but I'm sorry I said it."

"Bless your heart!" said Billy; "don't you worry over that, Peggy. That's all right. Incidentally, the things you've said to me and about me aren't true, of course, but we won't discuss that just now. I—I fancy we're both feeling a bit fagged. Go to bed, Peggy! We'll both go to bed, and the night will bring counsel, and we'll sleep off all unkindliness. Go to bed, little sister!—get all the beauty-sleep you aren't in the least in need of, and dream of how happy you're going to be with the man you love. And—and in the morning I may have something to say to you. Good-night, dear."

And this time he really went. And when he had come to the bend in the stairs his eyes turned back to hers, slowly and irresistibly, drawn toward them, as it seemed, just as the sunflower is drawn toward the sun, or the needle toward the pole, or, in fine, as the eyes of young gentlemen ordinarily are drawn toward the eyes of the one woman in the world. Then he disappeared.

The mummery of it vexed Margaret. There was no excuse for his looking at her in that way. It irritated her. She was almost as angry with him for doing it as she would have been for not doing it.

Therefore, she bent an angry face toward the fire, her mouth pouting in a rather inviting fashion. Then it rounded slowly into a sanguine O, which of itself suggested osculation, but in reality stood for "observe!" For the paper Billy had thrown into the fire had fallen under the gas-logs, and she remembered his guilty start.

"After all," said Margaret, "it's none of my business."

So she eyed it wistfully.

"It may be important," she considerately remembered. "It ought not to be left there."

So she fished it out with a big paper-cutter.

"But it can't be very important," she dissented afterward, "or he wouldn't have thrown it away."

So she looked at the superscripture on the back of it.

Then she gave a little gasp and tore it open and read it by the firelight.

Miss Hugonin subsequently took credit to herself for not going into hysterics. And I think she had some reason to; for she found the paper a duplicate of the one Billy had taken out of the secret drawer, with his name set in the place of hers. At the last Frederick R. Woods had relented toward his nephew.

Margaret laughed a little; then she cried a little; then she did both together. Afterward she sat in the firelight, very puzzled and very excited and very penitent and very beautiful, and was happier than she had ever been in her life.

"He had it in his pocket," her dear voice quavered; "he had it in his pocket, my brave, strong, beautiful Billy did, when he asked me to marry him. It was King Cophetua wooing the beggar-maid—and the beggar was an impudent, ungrateful, idiotic little *piece!*" Margaret hissed, in her most shrewish manner. "She ought to be spanked. She ought to go down on her knees to him in sackcloth, and tears, and ashes, and all sorts of penitential things. She will, too. Oh, it's such a beautiful world—*such* a beautiful world! Billy loves me—really! Billy's a millionaire, and I'm a pauper. Oh, I'm glad, glad, *glad!*"

She caressed the paper that had rendered the world such a goodly place to live in—caressed it tenderly and rubbed her cheek against it. That was Margaret's way of showing affection, you know; and I protest it must have been very pleasant for the paper. The only wonder was that the ink it was written in didn't turn red with delight.

Then she read it through again, for sheer enjoyment of those beautiful, incomprehensible words that disinherited her. How *lovely* of Uncle Fred! she thought. Of course, he'd forgiven Billy; who wouldn't? What beautiful language Uncle Fred used! quite prayer-booky, she termed it. Then she gasped.

The will in Billy's favour was dated a week earlier than the one they had found in the secret drawer. It was worthless, mere waste paper. At the last Frederick R. Woods's pride had conquered his love.

"Oh, the horrid old man!" Margaret wailed; "he's left me everything he had! How *dare* he disinherit Billy! I call it rank impertinence in him. Oh, boy dear, dear, *dear* boy!" Miss Hugonin crooned, in an ecstacy of tenderness and woe. "He found this first will in one of the other drawers, and thought *he* was the rich one, and came in a great whirl of joy to ask me to marry him, and I was horrid to him! Oh, what a mess I've made of it! I've called him a fortune-hunter, and I've told him I love another man, and he'll never, never ask me to marry him now. And I love him, I worship him, I adore him! And if only I were poor—"

Ensued a silence. Margaret lifted the two wills, scrutinised them closely, and then looked at the fire, interrogatively.

"It's penal servitude for quite a number of years," she said. "But, then, he really *couldn't* tell any one, you know. No gentleman would allow a lady to be locked up in jail. And if he knew—if he knew I didn't and couldn't consider him a fortune-hunter, I really believe he would—"

Whatever she believed he would do, the probability of his doing it seemed highly agreeable to Miss Hugonin. She smiled at the fire in the most friendly fashion, and held out one of the folded papers to it.

"Yes," said Margaret, "I'm quite sure he will."

There I think we may leave her. For I have dredged the dictionary, and I confess I have found no fitting words wherewith to picture this inconsistent, impulsive, adorable young woman, dreaming brave dreams in the firelight of her lover and of their united future. I should only bungle it. You must imagine it for yourself.

It is a pretty picture, is it not?—with its laughable side, perhaps; under the circumstances, whimsical, if you will; but very, very sacred. For she loved him with a clean heart, loved him infinitely.

Let us smile at it—tenderly—and pass on.

But upon my word, when I think of how unreasonably, how outrageously Margaret had behaved during the entire evening, I am tempted to depose her as our heroine. I begin to regret I had not selected Adèle Haggage.

She would have done admirably. For, depend upon it, she, too, had her trepidations, her white nights, her occult battles over Hugh Van Orden. Also, she was a pretty girl—if you care for brunettes—and accomplished. She was versed in I forget how many foreign languages, both Continental and dead, and could discourse sensibly in any one of them. She was perfectly reasonable, perfectly consistent, perfectly unimpulsive, and never expressed an opinion that was not countenanced by at least two competent authorities. I don't know a man living, prepared to dispute that Miss Haggage excelled Miss Hugonin in all these desirable qualities.

Yet with pleasing unanimity they went mad for Margaret and had the greatest possible respect for Adèle.

And, my dear Mrs. Grundy, I grant you cheerfully that this was all wrong. A sensible man, as you very justly observe, will seek in a woman something more enduring than mere personal attractions; he will value her for some sensible reason—say, for her wit, or her learning, or her skill in cookery, or her proficiency in Greek. A sensible man will look for a sensible woman; he will not concern his sensible head over such trumperies as a pair of bright eyes, or a red lip or so, or a satisfactory suit of hair. These are fleeting vanities.

However—

You have doubtless heard ere this, my dear madam, that had Cleopatra's nose been an inch shorter the destiny of the world would have been changed; had she been the woman you describe—perfectly reasonable, perfectly consistent, perfectly sensible in all she said and did—confess, dear lady, wouldn't Antony have taken to his heels and have fled from such a monster?

Chapter 14

I regret to admit that Mr. Woods did not toss feverishly about his bed all through the silent watches of the night. He was very miserable, but he was also twenty-six. That is an age when the blind bow-god deals no fatal wounds. It is an age to suffer poignantly, if you will; an age wherein to aspire to the dearest woman on earth, to write her halting verses, to lose her, to affect the *clichés* of cynicism, to hear the chimes at midnight—and after it all, to sleep like a top.

So Billy slept. And kind Hypnos loosed a dream through the gates of ivory that lifted him to a delectable land where Peggy was nineteen, and had never heard of Kennaston, and was unbelievably sweet and dear and beautiful. But presently they and the Colonel put forth to sea—on a great carved writing-desk—fishing for sharks, which the Colonel said were very plentiful in those waters; and Frederick R. Woods climbed up out of the sea, and said Billy was a fool and must go to college; and Peggy said that was impossible, as seventeen hundred and fifty thousand children had to be given an education apiece, and they couldn't spare one for Billy; and a missionary from Zambesi Land came out of one of the secret drawers and said Billy must give him both of his feet as he needed them for his working-girls' classes; and thereupon the sharks poked their heads out of the water and began, in a deafening chorus, to cry, "Feet, feet, feet!" And Billy then woke with a start, and found it was only the birds chattering in the dawn outside.

Then he was miserable.

He tossed, and groaned, and dozed, and smoked cigarettes until he could stand it no longer. He got up and dressed, in sheer desperation, and went for a walk in the gardens.

The day was clear as a new-minted coin. It was not yet wholly aired, not wholly free from the damp savour of night, but low in the east the sun was taking heart. A mile-long shadow footed it with Billy Woods in his pacings through the amber-chequered gardens. Actaeon-like, he surprised the world at its toilet, and its fleeting grace somewhat fortified his spirits.

But his thoughts pestered him like gnats. The things he said to the roses it is not necessary to set down.

Chapter 15

After a vituperative half-hour or so Mr. Woods was hungry. He came back toward Selwoode; and upon the terrace in front of the house he found Kathleen Saumarez.

During the warm weather, one corner of the terrace had been converted, by means of gay red-and-white awnings, into a sort of living-room. There were chairs, tables, sofa-cushions, bowls of roses, and any number of bright-coloured rugs. Altogether, it was a cosy place, and the glowing hues of its furnishings were very becoming to Mrs. Saumarez, who sat there writing industriously.

It was a thought embarrassing. They had avoided one another yesterday—rather obviously—both striving to put off a necessarily awkward meeting. Now it had come. And now, somehow, their eyes met for a moment, and they laughed frankly, and the awkwardness was gone.

"Kathleen," said Mr. Woods, with conviction, "you're a dear."

"You broke my heart," said she, demurely, "but I'm going to forgive you."

Mrs. Saumarez was not striving to be clever now. And, heavens (thought Billy), how much nicer she was like this! It wasn't the same woman: her thin cheeks flushed arbutus-like, and her rather metallic voice was grown low and gentle. Billy brought memories with him, you see; and for the moment, she was Kathleen Eppes again—Kathleen Eppes in the first flush of youth, eager, trustful, and joyous-hearted, as he had known her long ago. Since then, the poor woman had eaten of the bread of dependence and had found it salt enough; she had paid for it daily, enduring a thousand petty slights, a thousand petty insults, and smiling under them as only women can. But she had forgotten now that shrewd Kathleen Saumarez who must earn her livelihood as best she might. She smiled frankly—a purely unprofessional smile.

"I was sorry when I heard you were coming," she said, irrelevantly, "but I'm glad now."

Mr. Woods—I grieve to relate—was still holding her hand in his. There stirred in his pulses the thrill Kathleen Eppes had always wakened—a thrill of memory now, a mere wraith of emotion. He was thinking of a certain pink-cheeked girl with crinkly black-brown hair and eyes that he had likened to chrysoberyls—and he wondered whimsically what had become of her. This was not she. This was assuredly not Kathleen, for this woman had a large mouth—a humorous and kindly mouth it was true, but undeniably a large one—whereas, Kathleen's mouth had been quite perfect and rather diminutive than otherwise. Hadn't he rhymed of it often enough to know?

They stood gazing at one another for a long time; and in the back of Billy's brain lines of his old verses sang themselves to a sad little tune— the verses that reproved the idiocy of all other poets, who had very foolishly written their sonnets to other women: and yet, as the jingle pointed out,

> *Had these poets ever strayed*
> *In thy path, they had not made*
> *Random rhymes of Arabella,*
> *Songs of Dolly, hymns of Stella,*
> *Lays of Lalage or Chloris—*
> *Not of Daphne nor of Doris,*
> *Florimel nor Amaryllis,*
> *Nor of Phyllida nor Phyllis,*
> *Were their wanton melodies:*
> *But all of these—*
> *All their melodies had been*
> *Of thee, Kathleen.*

Would they have been? Billy thought it improbable. The verses were very silly; and, recalling the big, blundering boy who had written them, Billy began to wonder—somewhat forlornly—whither he, too, had vanished. He and the girl he had gone mad for both seemed rather mythical—legendary as King Pepin.

"Yes," said Mrs. Saumarez—and oh, she startled him; "I fancy they're both quite dead by now. Billy," she cried, earnestly, "don't laugh at them!—don't laugh at those dear, foolish children! I—somehow, I couldn't bear that, Billy."

"Kathleen," said Mr. Woods, in admiration, "you're a witch. I wasn't laughing, though, my dear. I was developing quite a twilight mood over them—a plaintive, old-lettery sort of mood, you know."

She sighed a little. "Yes—I know." Then her eyelids flickered in a parody of Kathleen's glance that Billy noted with a queer tenderness. "Come and talk to me, Billy," she commanded. "I'm an early bird this morning, and entitled to the very biggest and best-looking worm I can find. You're only a worm, you know—we're all worms. Mr. Jukesbury told me so last night, making an exception in my favour, for it appears I'm an angel. He was amorously inclined last night, the tipsy old fraud! It's shameless, Billy, the amount of money he gets out of Miss Hugonin—for the deserving poor. Do you know, I rather fancy he classes himself under that head? And I grant you he's poor enough—but deserving!" Mrs. Saumarez snapped her fingers eloquently.

"Eh? Shark, eh?" queried Mr. Woods, in some discomfort.

She nodded. "He is as bad as Sarah Haggage," she informed him, "and everybody knows what a bloodsucker she is. The Haggage is a disease, Billy, that all rich women are exposed to—'more easily caught than the pestilence, and the taker runs presently mad.' Depend upon it, Billy, those two will have every penny they can get out of your uncle's money."

"Peggy's so generous," he pleaded. "She wants to make everybody happy—bring about a general millenium, you know."

"She pays dearly enough for her fancies," said Mrs. Saumarez, in a hard voice. Then, after a little, she cried, suddenly: "Oh, Billy, Billy, it shames me to think of how we lie to her, and toady to her, and lead her on from one mad scheme to another!—all for the sake of the money we can pilfer incidentally! We're all arrant hypocrites, you know; I'm no better than the others, Billy—not a bit better. But my husband left me so poor, and I had always been accustomed to the pretty things of life, and I couldn't—I couldn't give them up, Billy. I love them too dearly. So I lie, and toady, and write drivelling talks about things I don't understand, for drivelling women to listen to, and I still have the creature comforts of life. I pawn my self-respect for them—that's all. Such a little price to pay, isn't it, Billy?"

She spoke in a sort of frenzy. I dare say that at the outset she wanted Mr. Woods to know the worst of her, knowing he could not fail to discover it in time. Billy brought memories with him, you see; and this shrewd, hard woman wanted, somehow, more than anything else in the world, that he should think well of her. So she babbled out the whole pitiful story, waiting in a kind of terror to see contempt and disgust awaken in his eyes.

But he merely said "I see—I see," very slowly, and his eyes were kindly. He couldn't be angry with her, somehow; that pink-cheeked, crinkly haired girl stood between them and shielded her. He was only very, very sorry.

"And Kennaston?" he asked, after a little.

Mrs. Saumarez flushed. "Mr. Kennaston is a man of great genius," she said, quickly. "Of course, Miss Hugonin is glad to assist him in publishing his books—it's an honour to her that he permits it. They have to be published privately, you know, as the general public isn't capable of appreciating such dainty little masterpieces. Oh, don't make any mistake, Billy—Mr. Kennaston is a very wonderful and very admirable man."

"H'm, yes; he struck me as being an unusually nice chap," said Mr. Woods, untruthfully. "I dare say they'll be very happy."

"Who?" Mrs. Saumarez demanded.

"Why—er—I don't suppose they'll make any secret of it," Billy stammered, in tardy repentance of his hasty speaking. "Peggy told me last night she had accepted him."

Mrs. Saumarez turned to rearrange a bowl of roses. She seemed to have some difficulty over it.

"Billy," she spoke, inconsequently, and with averted head, "an honest man is the noblest work of God—and the rarest."

Billy groaned.

"Do you know," said he, "I've just been telling the roses in the gardens yonder the same thing about women? I'm a misogynist this morning. I've decided no woman is worthy of being loved."

"That is quite true," she assented, "but, on the other hand, no man is worthy of loving."

Billy smiled.

"I've likewise come to the conclusion," said he, "that a man's love is like his hat, in that any peg will do to hang it on; also, in that the proper and best place for it is on his own head. Oh, I assure you, I vented any number of cheap cynicisms on the helpless roses! And yet—will you believe it, Kathleen?—it doesn't seem to make me feel a bit better—no, not a bit."

"It's very like his hat," she declared, "in that he has a new one every year." Then she rested her hand on his, in a half-maternal fashion. "What's the matter, boy?" she asked, softly. "You're always so fresh and wholesome. I don't like to see you like this. Better leave phrase-making to us phrase-mongers."

Her voice rang true—true, and compassionate, and tender, and all that a woman's voice should be. Billy could not but trust her.

"I've been an ass," said he, rather tragically. "Oh, not an unusual ass, Kathleen—just the sort men are always making of themselves. You see, before I went to France, there was a girl I—cared for. And I let a quarrel come between us—a foolish, trifling, idle little quarrel, Kathleen, that we might have made up in a half-hour. But I was too proud, you see. No, I wasn't proud, either," Mr. Woods amended, bitterly; "I was simply pig-headed and mulish. So I went away. And yesterday I saw her again and realised that I—still cared. That's all, Kathleen. It isn't an unusual story." And Mr. Woods laughed, mirthlessly, and took a turn on the terrace.

Mrs. Saumarez was regarding him intently. Her cheeks were of a deeper, more attractive pink, and her breath came and went quickly.

"I—I don't understand," she said, in a rather queer voice.

"Oh, it's simple enough," Billy assured her. "You see, she—well, I think she would have married me once. Yes, she cared for me once. And I quarreled with her—I, conceited young ass that I was, actually presumed to dictate to the dearest, sweetest, most lovable woman on earth, and tell her what she must do and what she mustn't. I!—good Lord, I, who wasn't worthy to sweep a crossing clean for her!—who wasn't worthy to breathe the same air with her!—who wasn't worthy to exist in the same world she honoured by living in! Oh, I *was* an ass! But I've paid for it!—oh, yes, Kathleen, I've paid dearly for it, and I'll pay more dearly yet before I've done. I tried to avoid her yesterday—you must have seen that. And I couldn't—I give you my word, I could no more have kept away from her than I could have spread a pair of wings and flown away. She doesn't care a bit for me now; but I can no more give up loving her than I can give up eating my dinner. That isn't a pretty simile, Kathleen, but it expresses the way I feel toward her. It isn't merely that I want her; it's more than that—oh, far more than that. I simply can't do without her. Don't you understand, Kathleen?" he asked, desperately.

"Yes—I think I understand," she said, when he had ended. "I—oh, Billy, I am almost sorry. It's dear of you—dear of you, Billy, to care for me still, but—but I'm almost sorry you care so much. I'm not worth it, boy dear. And I—I really don't know what to say. You must let me think."

Mr. Woods gave an inarticulate sound. The face she turned to him was perplexed, half-sad, fond, a little pleased, and strangely compassionate. It was Kathleen Eppes who sat beside him; the six years were as utterly forgotten as the name of Magdalen's first lover. She was a girl again, listening—with a heart that fluttered, I dare say—to the wild talk, the mad dithyrambics of a big, blundering boy.

The ludicrous horror of it stunned Mr. Woods.

He could no more have told her of her mistake than he could have struck her in the face.

"Kathleen—!" said he, vaguely.

"Let me think!—ah, let me think, Billy!" she pleaded, in a flutter of joy and amazement. "Go away, boy dear!—Go away for a little and let me think! I'm not an emotional woman, but I'm on the verge of hysterics now, for—for several reasons. Go in to breakfast, Billy! I—I want to be alone. You've made me very proud and—and sorry, I think, and glad, and—and—oh, I don't know, boy dear. But please go now—please!"

Billy went.

In the living-hall he paused to inspect a picture with peculiar interest. Since Kathleen cared for him (he thought, rather forlornly), he must perjure himself in as plausible a manner as might be possible; please God, having done what he had done, he would lie to her like a gentleman and try to make her happy.

A vision in incredible violet ruffles, coming down to breakfast, saw him, and paused on the stairway, and flushed and laughed deliciously.

Poor Billy stared at her; and his heart gave a great bound and then appeared to stop for an indefinite time.

"Good Lord!" said Mr. Woods, in his soul. "And I thought I was an ass last night! Why, last night, in comparison, I displayed intelligence that was almost human! Oh, Peggy, Peggy! if I only dared tell you what I think of you, I believe I would gladly die afterward—yes, I'm sure I would. You really haven't any right to be so beautiful!—it isn't fair to us, Peggy!"

But the vision was peeping over the bannisters at him, and the vision's eyes were sparkling with a lucent mischief and a wonderful, half-hushed contralto was demanding of him:

> *"Oh, where have you been, Billy boy, Billy boy?*
> *Oh, where have you been, charming Billy?"*

And Billy's baritone answered her:

> *"I've been to seek a wife—"*

and broke off in a groan.

"Good Lord!" said Mr. Woods.

It was a ludicrous business, if you will. Indeed, it was vastly humorous—was it not?—this woman's thinking a man's love might by any chance endure through six whole years. But their love endures, you see; and the silly creatures have a superstition among them that love is a sacred thing, stronger than time, victorious over death itself. Let us laugh, then, at Kathleen Saumarez—those of us who have learned that love is only a tinkling cymbal and faith a sounding brass and fidelity an obsolete affectation: but for my part, I honour and think better of the woman who through all her struggles with the world—through all those sordid, grim, merciless, secret battles where the vanquished may not even cry for succour—I honour her, I say, for that she had yet cherished the memory of that first love which is the best and purest and most unselfish and most excellent thing in life.

Chapter 16

B reakfast Margaret enjoyed hugely. I regret to confess that the fact that every one of her guests was more or less miserable moved this hard-hearted young woman to untimely and excessive mirth. Only Mrs. Saumarez puzzled her, for she could think of no reason for that lady's manifest agitation when Kathleen eventually joined the others.

But for the rest, the hopeless glances that Hugh Van Orden cast toward her caused Adèle to flush, and Mrs. Haggage to become despondent and speechless and astonishingly rigid; and Petheridge Jukesbury's vaguely apologetic attitude toward the world struck Miss Hugonin as infinitely diverting. Kennaston she pitied a little; but his bearing toward her ranged ludicrously from that of proprietorship to that of supplication, and, moreover, she was furious with him for having hinted at various times that Billy was a fortune-hunter.

Margaret was quite confident by this that she had never believed him—"not really, you know"—having argued the point out at some length the night before, and reaching her conclusion by a course of reasoning peculiar to herself.

Mr. Woods, as you may readily conceive, was sunk in the Slough of Despond deeper than ever plummet sounded. Margaret thought this very nice of him; it was a delicate tribute to her that he ate nothing; and the fact that Hugh Van Orden and Petheridge Jukesbury—as she believed—acted in precisely the same way for precisely the same reason, merely demonstrated, of course, their overwhelming conceit and presumption.

So sitting in the great Eagle's shadow, she ate a quantity of marmalade—she was wont to begin the day in this ungodly English fashion—and gossiped like a brook trotting over sunlit pebbles. She had planned a pulverising surprise for the house-party; and in due time, she intended to explode it, and subsequently Billy was to apologise for his conduct, and then they were to live happily ever afterward.

She had not yet decided what he was to apologise for; that was his affair. His conscience ought to have told him, by this, wherein he had offended; and if his conscience hadn't, why then, of course, he would have to apologise for his lack of proper sensibility.

After breakfast she went, according to her usual custom, to her father's rooms, for, as I think I have told you, the old gentleman was never visible until noon. She had astonishing news for him.

What time she divulged it, the others sat on the terrace, and Mr. Kennaston read to them, as he had promised, from his "Defense of Ignorance." It proved a welcome diversion to more than one of the party. Mr. Woods, especially, esteemed it a godsend; it staved off misfortune for at least a little; so he sat at Kathleen's side in silence, trying desperately to be happy, trying desperately not to see the tiny wrinkles, the faint crow's feet Time had sketched in her face as a memorandum of the work he meant to do shortly.

Billy consoled himself with the reflection that he was very fond of her; but, oh (he thought), what worship, what adoration he could accord this woman if she would only decline—positively—to have anything whatever to do with him!

I think we ought not to miss hearing Mr. Kennaston's discourse. It is generally conceded that his style is wonderfully clever; and I have no doubt that his detractors—who complain that his style is mere word-twisting, a mere inversion of the most ancient truisms—are actuated by the very basest jealousy. Let us listen, then, and be duly edified as he reads in a low, sweet voice, and the birds twitter about him in the clear morning.

"It has been for many years," Mr. Kennaston began, "the custom of patriotic gentlemen in quest of office to point with pride to the fact that the schoolmaster is abroad in the land, in whose defense they stand pledged to draw their salaries and fight to the last gasp for reelection. These lofty platitudes, while trying to the lungs, doubtless appeal to a certain class of minds. But, indeed, the schoolmaster is not abroad; he is domesticated in every village in America, where each hamlet has its would-be Shakespeare, and each would-be Shakespeare has his 'Hamlet' by heart. Learning is rampant in the land, and valuable information is pasted up in the streetcars so that he who rides may read.

"And Ignorance—beautiful, divine Ignorance—is forsaken by a generation that clamours for the truth. And what value, pray, has this Truth that we should lust after it?"

He glanced up, in an inquiring fashion. Mr. Jukesbury, meeting his eye, smiled and shook his head and said "Fie, fie!" very placidly.

To do him justice, he had not the least idea what Kennaston was talking about.

"I am aware," the poet continued, with an air of generosity, "that many pleasant things have been said of it. In fact, our decade has turned its back relentlessly upon the decayed, and we no longer read the lament over the lost art of lying issued many magazines ago by a once prominent British author. Still, without advancing any Wilde theories, one may fairly claim that truth is a jewel—a jewel with many facets, differing in appearance from each point of view.

"And while 'Tell the truth and shame the Devil' is a very pretty sentiment, it need not necessarily mean anything. The Devil, if there be a personal devil—and it has been pointed out, with some show of reason, that an impersonal one could scarcely carry out such enormous contracts—would, in all probability, rather approve than otherwise of indiscriminate truth-telling. Irritation is the root of all evil; and there is nothing more irritating than to hear the truth about one's self. It is bad enough, in all conscience, to be insulted, but the truth of an insult is the barb that prevents its retraction. 'Truth hurts' has all the pathos of understatement. It not only hurts, but infuriates. It has no more right to go naked in public than any one else. Indeed, it has less right; for truth-telling is natural to mankind—as is shown by its prevalence among the younger sort, such as children and cynics—and, as Shakespeare long ago forgot to tell us, a touch of nature makes the whole world embarrassed."

At this point Mrs. Haggage sniffed. She considered he was growing improper. She distrusted Nature.

"Truth-telling, then, may safely be regarded as an unamiable indiscretion. In art, the bare truth must, in common gallantry, be awarded a print petticoat or one of canvas, as the case may be, to hide her nakedness; and in life, it is a disastrous virtue that we have united to commend and avoid. Nor is the decision an unwise one; for man is a gregarious animal, knowing that friendship is, at best, but a feeble passion and therefore to be treated with the care due an invalid. It is impossible to be quite candid in conversation with a man; and with a woman it is absolutely necessary that your speech should be candied.

"Truth, then, is the least desirable of acquaintances.

"But even if one wished to know the truth, the desire could scarcely be fulfilled. Francis Bacon, Lord Verulam, a prominent lawyer of Elizabeth's time, who would have written Shakespeare's plays had his other occupations not prevented it, quotes Pilate as inquiring, 'What is Truth?'—and then not staying for an answer. Pilate deserves all the praise he has never received. Nothing is quite true. Even Truth lies at the bottom of a well and not infrequently in other places. No assertion is one whit truer than its opposite."

A mild buzz of protest rose about him. Kennaston smiled and cocked his head on one side.

"We have, for example," he pointed out, "a large number of proverbs, the small coin of conversation, received everywhere, whose value no one disputes. They are rapped forth, like an oath, with an air of settling the question once and forever. Well! there is safety in quotations. But even the Devil can cite Shakespeare for his purpose. 'Never put off till to-morrow what you can do to-day' agrees ill with 'Sufficient unto the day is the evil thereof'; and it is somewhat difficult to reconcile 'Take care of the pence, and the pounds will take care of themselves' with the equally familiar 'Penny-wise, pound-foolish.' Yet the sayings are equally untrue; any maxim is, perforce, a general statement, and therefore fallacious, and therefore universally accepted. Art is long, and life is short, but the platitudes concerning them are both insufferable and eternal. We must remember that a general statement is merely a snap-shot at flying truth, an instantaneous photograph of a moving body. It may be the way that a thing is; but it is never the way in which any one ever saw that thing, or ever will. This is, of course, a general statement.

"As to present events, then, it may be assumed that no one is either capable or desirous of speaking the truth; why, then, make such a pother about it as to the past? There we have carried the investigation of truth to such an extreme that nowadays very few of us dare believe anything. Opinions are difficult to secure when a quarter of an hour in the library will prove either side of any question. Formerly, people had a few opinions, which, if erroneous, were at least universal. Nero was not considered an immaculate man. The Flood was currently believed to have caused the death of quite a number of persons. And George Washington, it was widely stated, once cut down a cherry-tree. But now all these comfortable illusions have been destroyed by 'the least little men who spend their time and lose their wits in chasing nimble and retiring truth, to the extreme perturbation and drying up of the moistures.'"

Kennaston looked up for a moment, and Billy Woods, who had counted seven wrinkles and was dropping into a forlorn doze, started violently. His interest then became abnormal.

"There are," Mr. Kennaston complained, rather reproachfully, "too many inquiries, doubts, investigations, discoveries, and apologies. There are palliations of Tiberius, eulogies of Henry VIII, rehabilitations of Aaron Burr. Lucretia Borgia, it appears, was a grievously misunderstood woman, and Heliogabalus a most exemplary monarch; even the dog in the manger may have been a nervous animal in search of rest and quiet. As for Shakespeare, he was an atheist, a syndicate, a lawyer's clerk, an inferior writer, a Puritan, a scholar, a *nom de plume*, a doctor of medicine, a fool, a poacher, and another man of the same name. Information of this sort crops up on every side. Even the newspapers are infected; truth lurks in the patent-medicine advertisements, and sometimes creeps stealthily into the very editorials. We must all learn the true facts of history, whether we will or no; eventually, the writers of historical romance will not escape.

"So the sad tale goes. Ignorance—beautiful, divine Ignorance—is forsaken by a generation that clamours for the truth. The earnest-minded person has plucked Zeus out of Heaven, and driven the Maenad from the wood, and dragged Poseidon out of his deep-sea palace. The conclaves of Olympus, it appears, are merely nature-myths; the stately legends clustering about them turn out to be a rather elaborate method of expressing the fact that it occasionally rains. The heroes who endured their angers and jests and tragic loves are delicately veiled allusions to the sun—surely, a very harmless topic of conversation, even in Greece; and the monsters, 'Gorgons and Hydras and Chimæras dire,' their grisly offspring, their futile opponents, are but personified frosts. Mythology—the poet's necessity, the fertile mother of his inventions—has become a series of atmospheric phenomena, and the labours of Hercules prove to be a dozen weather bulletins.

"Is it any cause for wonder, that under this cheerless influence our poetry is either silent or unsold? The true poet must be ignorant, for information is the thief of rhyme. And it is only in dealing with—"

Kennaston paused. Margaret had appeared in the vestibule, and behind her stood her father, looking very grave.

"We have made a most interesting discovery," Miss Hugonin airily announced to the world at large. "It appears that Uncle Fred left all his property to Mr. Woods here. We found the will only last night. I'm sure you'll all be interested to learn I'm a pauper now, and intend to support myself by plain sewing. Any work of this nature you may choose to favour me with, ladies and gentlemen, will receive my most *earnest* attention."

She dropped a courtesy. The scene appealed to her taste for the dramatic.

Billy came toward her quickly.

"Peggy," he demanded of her, in the semi-privacy of the vestibule, "will you kindly elucidate the meaning of this da—this idiotic foolishness?"

"Why, this," she explained, easily, and exhibited a folded paper. "I found it in the grate last night."

He inspected it with large eyes. "That's absurd," he said, at length. "You know perfectly well this will isn't worth the paper it's written on."

"My dear sir," she informed him, coldly, "you are vastly mistaken. You see, I've burned the other one." She pushed by him. "Mr. Kennaston, are you ready for our walk? We'll finish the paper some other time. Wasn't it the strangest thing in the world—?" Her dear, deep, mellow voice died away as she and Kennaston disappeared in the gardens.

Billy gasped.

But meanwhile, Colonel Hugonin had given the members of his daughter's house-party some inkling as to the present posture of affairs. They were gazing at Billy Woods rather curiously. He stood in the vestibule of Selwoode, staring after Margaret Hugonin; but they stared at him, and over his curly head, sculptured above the door-way, they saw the Eagle—the symbol of the crude, incalculable power of wealth.

Mr. Woods stood in the vestibule of his own house.

Chapter 17

B y gad!" said Colonel Hugonin, very grimly, "anybody would think you'd just lost a fortune instead of inheriting one! Wish you joy of it, Billy. I ain't saying, you know, we shan't miss it, my daughter and I— no, begad, for it's a nice pot of money, and we'll miss it damnably. But since somebody had to have it, I'd much rather it was you, my boy, than a set of infernal, hypocritical, philanthropic sharks, and I'm damn' glad Frederick has done the square thing by you—yes, begad!"

The old gentleman was standing beside Mr. Woods in the vestibule of Selwoode, some distance from the other members of the house-party, and was speaking in confidence. He was sincere; I don't say that the thought of facing the world at sixty-five with practically no resources save his half-pay—I think I have told you that the Colonel's diversions had drunk up his wife's fortune and his own like a glass of water—I don't say that this thought moved him to hilarity. Over it, indeed, he pulled a frankly grave face.

But he cared a deal for Billy; and even now there was balm— soothing, priceless balm—to be had of the reflection that this change in his prospects affected materially the prospects of those cultured, broad-minded, philanthropic persons who had aforetime set his daughter to requiring of him a perusal of Herbert Spencer.

Billy was pretty well aware how monetary matters stood with the old wastrel; and the sincerity of the man affected him far more than the most disinterested sentiments would have done. Mr. Woods accordingly shook hands, with entirely unnecessary violence.

"You're a trump, that's what you are!" he declared; "oh, yes, you are, Colonel! You're an incorrigible, incurable old ace of trumps—the very best there is in the pack—and it's entirely useless for you to attempt to conceal it."

"Gad——!" said the Colonel.

"And don't you worry about that will," Mr. Woods advised. "I—I can't explain things just now, but it's all right. You just wait—just wait till I've seen Peggy," Billy urged, in desperation, "and I'll explain everything."

"By gad——!" said the Colonel. But Mr. Woods was half-way out of the vestibule.

Mr. Woods was in an unenviable state of perturbation.

He could not quite believe that Peggy had destroyed the will; the thing out-Heroded Herod, out-Margareted Margaret. But if she had, it struck him as a high-handed proceeding, entailing certain vague penalties made and provided by the law to cover just such cases—penalties of whose nature he was entirely ignorant and didn't care to think. Heavens! for all he knew, that angel might have let herself in for a jail sentence.

Billy pictured that queen among women! that paragon! with her glorious hair cropped and her pink-tipped little hands set to beating hemp—he had a shadowy notion that the lives of all female convicts were devoted to this pursuit—and groaned in horror.

"In the name of Heaven!" Mr. Woods demanded of his soul, "what *possible* reason could she have had for this new insanity? And in the name of Heaven, why couldn't she have put off her *tête-à-tête* with Kennaston long enough to explain? And in the name of Heaven, what does she see to admire in that putty-faced, grimacing ass, any way! And in the name of Heaven, what am I to say to this poor, old man here? I can't explain that his daughter isn't in any danger of being poor, but merely of being locked up in jail! And in the name of Heaven, how long does that outrageous angel expect me to remain in this state of suspense!"

Billy groaned again and paced the vestibule. Then he retraced his steps, shook hands with Colonel Hugonin once more, and, Kennaston or no Kennaston, set out to find her.

Chapter 18

B ut when he came out upon the terrace, Sarah Ellen Haggage stopped him—stopped him with a queer blending of diffidence and resolve in her manner.

The others, by this, had disappeared in various directions, puzzled and exceedingly uncertain what to do. Indeed, to congratulate Billy in the Colonel's presence would have been tactless; and, on the other hand, to condole with the Colonel without seeming to affront the wealthy Mr. Woods was almost impossible. So they temporised and fled—all save Mrs. Haggage.

She, alone, remained to view Mr. Woods with newly opened eyes; for as he paused impatiently—the sculptured Eagle above his head— she perceived that he was a remarkably handsome and intelligent young man. Her motherly heart opened toward this lonely, wealthy orphan.

"My dear Billy," she cooed, with asthmatic gentleness, "as an old, old friend of your mother's, aren't you going to let me tell you how rejoiced Adèle and I are over your good fortune? It isn't polite, you naughty boy, for you to run away from your friends as soon as they've heard this wonderful news. Ah, such news it was—such a manifest intervention of Providence! My heart has been fluttering, fluttering like a little bird, Billy, ever since I heard it."

In testimony to this fact, Mrs. Haggage clasped a stodgy hand to an exceedingly capacious bosom, and exhibited the whites of her eyes freely. Her smile, however, remained unchanged and ample.

"Er—ah—oh, yes! Very kind of you, I'm sure!" said Mr. Woods.

"I never in my life saw Adèle so deeply affected by *anything*," Mrs. Haggage continued, with a certain large archness. "The sweet child was always so fond of you, you know, Billy. Ah, I remember distinctly hearing her speak of you many and many a time when you were in that dear, delightful, wicked Paris, and wonder when you would come back to your friends—not very grand and influential friends, Billy, but sincere, I trust, for all that."

Mr. Woods said he had no doubt of it.

"So many people," she informed him, confidentially, "will pursue you with adulation now that you are wealthy. Oh, yes, you will find that wealth makes a great difference, Billy. But not with Adèle and me—no, dear boy, despise us if you will, but my child and I are not mercenary.

Money makes no difference with us; we shall be the same to you that we always were—sincerely interested in your true welfare, overjoyed at your present good fortune, prayerful as to your brilliant future, and delighted to have you drop in any evening to dinner. We do not consider money the chief blessing of life; no, don't tell me that most people are different, Billy, for I know it very well, and many is the tear that thought has cost me. We live in a very mercenary world, my dear boy; but *our* thoughts, at least, are set on higher things, and I trust we can afford to despise the merely temporal blessings of life, and I entreat you to remember that our humble dwelling is always open to the son of my old, old friend, and that there is always a jug of good whiskey in the cupboard."

Thus in the shadow of the Eagle babbled the woman whom—for all her absurdities—Margaret had loved as a mother.

Billy thanked her with an angry heart.

"And this"—I give you the gist of his meditations—"this is Peggy's dearest friend! Oh, Philanthropy, are thy protestations, then, all void and empty, and are thy noblest sentiments—every one of 'em—so full of sound and rhetoric, so specious, so delectable—are these, then, but dicers' oaths!"

Aloud, "I'm rather surprised, you know," he said, slowly, "that you take it just this way, Mrs. Haggage. I should have thought you'd have been sorry on—on Miss Hugonin's account. It's awfully jolly of you, of course—oh, awfully jolly, and I appreciate it at its true worth, I assure you. But it's a bit awkward, isn't it, that the poor girl will be practically penniless? I really don't know whom she'll turn to now."

Then Billy, the diplomatist, received a surprise.

"She'll come with me, of course," said Mrs. Haggage.

Mr. Woods made an—unfortunately—inaudible observation.

"I beg your pardon?" she queried. Then, obtaining no response, she continued, with perfect simplicity: "Margaret's quite like a daughter to me, you know. Of course, she and the Colonel will come with us— at least, until affairs are a bit more settled. Even afterward—well, we have a large house, Billy, and I don't see that they'd be any better off anywhere else."

Billy's emotions were complex.

"You big-hearted old parasite," his own heart was singing. "If you could only keep that ring of truth that's in your voice for your platform utterances—why, in less than no time you could afford to feed your Afro-Americans on nightingales' tongues and clothe every working-girl in the land in cloth of gold! You've been pilfering from Peggy for years—pilfering right and left with both hands! But you've loved her all the time, God bless you; and now the moment she's in trouble you're ready to take both her and the Colonel—whom, by the way, you must very cordially detest—and share your pitiful, pilfered little crusts with 'em and—having two more mouths to feed—probably pilfer a little more outrageously in the future! You're a sanctimonious old hypocrite, you are, and a pious fraud, and a delusion, and a snare, and you and Adèle have nefarious designs on me at this very moment, but I think I'd like to kiss you!"

Indeed, I believe Mr. Woods came very near doing so. She loved Peggy, you see; and he loved every one who loved her.

But he compromised by shaking hands energetically, for a matter of five minutes, and entreating to be allowed to subscribe to some of her deserving charitable enterprises—any one she might mention—and so left the old lady a little bewildered, but very much pleased.

She decided that for the future Adèle must not see so much of Mr. Van Orden. She began to fear that gentleman's views of life were not sufficiently serious.

Chapter 19

B illy went into the gardens in pursuit of Margaret. He was almost
happy now and felt vaguely ashamed of himself. Then he came
upon Kathleen Saumarez, who, indeed, was waiting for him there; and
his heart went down into his boots.

He realised on a sudden that he was one of the richest men in
America. It was a staggering thought. Also, Mr. Woods's views,
at this moment, as to the advantages of wealth, might have been
interesting.

Kathleen stood silent for an instant, eyes downcast, face flushed.
She was trembling.

Then, "Billy," she asked, almost inaudibly, "do—do you still want—
your answer?"

The birds sang about them. Spring triumphed in the gardens. She
looked very womanly and very pretty.

To all appearances, it might easily have been a lover and his lass
met in the springtide, shamefaced after last night's kissing. But Billy,
somehow, lacked much of the elation and the perfect content and the
disposition to burst into melody that is currently supposed to seize
upon rustic swains at such moments. He merely wanted to know if at
any time in the remote future his heart would be likely to resume the
discharge of its proper functions. It was standing still now.

However, "Can you ask—dear?" His words, at least, lied gallantly.

The poor woman looked up into Billy's face. After years of battling
with the world, here for the asking was peace and luxury and wealth
incalculable, and—as Kathleen thought—a love that had endured since
they were boy and girl together. Yet she shrunk from him a little and
clinched her hands before she spoke.

"Yes," Kathleen faltered, and afterward she shuddered.

And here, if for the moment I may prefigure the Eagle as a sentient
being, I can imagine his chuckle.

"Please God," thought poor Billy, "I will make her happy. Yes, please
God, I can at least do that, since she cares for me."

Then he kissed her.

"My dear," said he, aloud, "I'll try to make you happy. And—and you
don't mind, do you, if I leave you now?" queried this ardent lover. "You
see, it's absolutely necessary I should see—see Miss Hugonin about this

will business. You don't mind very much, do you—darling?" Mr. Woods inquired of her, the last word being rather obviously an afterthought.

"No," said she. "Not if you must—dear."

Billy went away, lugging a heart of lead in his breast.

Kathleen stared after him and gave a hard, wringing motion of her hands. She had done what many women do daily; the thing is common and sensible and universally commended; but in her own eyes, the draggled trollop of the pavements was neither better nor worse than she.

At the entrance of the next walkway Billy encountered Felix Kennaston—alone and in the most ebulliently mirthful of humours.

Chapter 20

B ut we had left Mr. Kennaston, I think, in company with Miss
Hugonin, at the precise moment she inquired of him whether it
were not the strangest thing in the world—referring thereby to the
sudden manner in which she had been disinherited.

The poet laughed and assented. Afterward, turning north from
the front court, they descended past the shield-bearing griffins—and
you may depend upon it that each shield is adorned with a bas-relief
of the Eagle—that guard the broad stairway leading to the formal
gardens of Selwoode. The gardens stretch northward to the confines
of Peter Blagden's estate of Gridlington; and for my part—unless
it were that primitive garden that Adam lost—I can imagine no
goodlier place.

On this particular forenoon, however, neither Miss Hugonin nor
Felix Kennaston had eyes for its comeliness; silently they braved the
griffins, and in silence they skirted the fish-pond—silver-crinkling in
the May morning—and passed through cloistral ilex-shadowed walks,
and amphitheatres of green velvet, and terraces ample and mellow in
the sunlight, silently. The trees pelted them with blossoms; pedestaled
in leafy recesses, Satyrs grinned at them apishly, and the arrows of
divers pot-bellied Cupids threatened them, and Fauns piped for them
ditties of no tone; the birds were about shrill avocations overhead, and
everywhere the heatless, odourful air was a caress; but for all this, Miss
Hugonin and Mr. Kennaston were silent and very fidgetty.

Margaret was hatless—and the glory of the eminently sensible spring
sun appeared to centre in her hair—and violet-clad; and the gown, like
most of her gowns, was all tiny tucks and frills and flounces, diapered
with semi-transparencies—unsubstantial, foam-like, mere violet froth.
As she came starry-eyed through the gardens, the impudent wind trifling
with her hair, I protest she might have been some lady of Oberon's court
stolen out of Elfland to bedevil us poor mortals, with only a moonbeam
for the changeable heart of her, and for raiment a violet shadow spirited
from the under side of some big, fleecy cloud.

They came presently through a trim, yew-hedged walkway to a
summer-house covered with vines, into which Margaret peeped and
declined to enter, on the ground that it was entirely too chilly and gloomy
and *exactly* like a mausoleum; but nearby they found a semi-circular

marble bench about which a group of elm-trees made a pleasant shadow splashed at just the proper intervals with sunlight.

On this Margaret seated herself; and then pensively moved to the other end of the bench, because a slanting sunbeam fell there. Since it was absolutely necessary to blast Mr. Kennaston's dearest hopes, she thoughtfully endeavoured to distract his attention from his own miseries—as far as might be possible—by showing him how exactly like an aureole her hair was in the sunlight. Margaret always had a kind heart.

Kennaston stood before her, smiling a little. He was the sort of man to appreciate the manoeuver.

"My lady," he asked, very softly, "haven't you any good news for me on this wonderful morning?"

"Excellent news," Margaret assented, with a cheerfulness that was not utterly free from trepidation. "I've decided not to marry you, beautiful, and I trust you're properly grateful. You see, you're very nice, of course, but I'm going to marry somebody else, and bigamy is a crime, you know; and, anyhow, I'm only a pauper, and you'd never be able to put up with my temper—now, beautiful, I'm quite sure you couldn't, so there's not a bit of use in arguing it. Some day you'd end by strangling me, which would be horribly disagreeable for me, and then they'd hang you for it, you know, and that would be equally disagreeable for you. Fancy, though, what a good advertisement it would be for your poems!"

She was not looking at him now—oh, no, Margaret was far too busily employed getting the will (which she had carried all this time) into an absurd little silver chain-bag hanging at her waist. She had no time to look at Felix Kennaston. There was such scant room in the bag; her purse took up so much space there was scarcely any left for the folded paper; the affair really required her closest, undivided attention. Besides, she had not the least desire to look at Kennaston just now.

"Beautiful child," he pleaded, "look at me!"

But she didn't.

She felt that at that moment she could have looked at a gorgon, say, or a cockatrice, or any other trifle of that nature with infinitely greater composure. The pause that followed Margaret accordingly devoted to a scrutiny of his shoes and sincere regret that their owner was not a mercenary man who would be glad to be rid of her.

"Beautiful child," spoke the poet's voice, sadly, "you aren't—surely, you aren't saying this in mistaken kindness to me? Surely, you aren't saying this because of what has happened in regard to your money

JAMES BRANCH CABELL

affairs? Believe me, my dear, that makes no difference to me. It is you I love—you, the woman of my heart—and not a certain, and doubtless desirable, amount of metal disks and dirty paper."

"Now I suppose you're going to be very noble and very nasty about it," observed Miss Hugonin, resentfully. "That's my main objection to you, you know, that you haven't any faults I can recognise and feel familiar and friendly with."

"My dear," he protested, "I assure you I am not intentionally disagreeable."

At that, she raised velvet eyes to his—with a visible effort, though—and smiled.

"I know you far too well to think that," she said, wistfully. "I know I'm not worthy of you. I'm tremendously fond of you, beautiful, but—but, you see, I love somebody else," Margaret concluded, with admirable candour.

"Ah!" said he, in a rather curious voice. "The painter chap, eh?"

Then Margaret's face flamed in a wonderful glow of shame and happiness and pride that must have made the surrounding roses very hopelessly jealous. A quaint mothering look, sacred, divine, Madonna-like, woke in her great eyes as she thought—remorsefully—of how unhappy Billy must be at that very moment and of how big he was and of his general niceness; and she desired, very heartily, that this fleshy young man would make his scene and have done with it. Who was he, forsooth, to keep her from Billy? She wished she had never heard of Felix Kennaston.

Souvent femme varie, my brothers.

However, "Yes," said Margaret..

"You are a dear," said Mr. Kennaston, with conviction in his voice.

I dare say Margaret was surprised.

But the poet had taken her hand and had kissed it reverently, and then sat down beside her, twisting one foot under him in a fashion he had. He was frankly grateful to her for refusing him; and, the mask of affectation slipped, she saw in him another man.

"I am an out-and-out fraud," he confessed, with the gayest of smiles. "I am not in love with you, and I am inexpressibly glad that you are not in love with me. Oh, Margaret, Margaret—you don't mind if I call you that, do you? I shall have to, in any event, because I like you so tremendously now that we are not going to be married—you have no idea what a night I spent."

"I consider it most peculiar and unsympathetic of my hair not to have turned gray. I thought you were going to have me, you see."

Margaret was far to much astonished to be angry.

"But last night!" she presently echoed, in candid surprise. "Why, last night you didn't know I was poor!"

He wagged a protesting forefinger. "That made no earthly difference," he assured her. "Of course, it was the money—and in some degree the moon—that induced me to make love to you. I acted on the impulse of the moment; just for an instant, the novelty of doing a perfectly sensible thing—and marrying money is universally conceded to come under that head—appealed to me. So I did it. But all the time I was in love with Kathleen Saumarez. Why, the moment I left you, I began to realise that not even you—and you are quite the most fascinating and generally adorable woman I ever knew, Margaret—I began to realise, I say, that not even you could ever make me forget that fact. And I was very properly miserable. It is extremely queer," Mr. Kennaston continued, after an interval of meditation, "but falling in love appears to be the one utterly inexplicable, utterly reasonless thing one ever does in one's life. You can usually think of some more or less plausible palliation for embezzlement, say, or for robbing a cathedral or even for committing suicide—but no man can ever explain how he happened to fall in love. He simply did it."

Margaret nodded sagely. She knew.

"Now you," Mr. Kennaston was pleased to say, "are infinitely more beautiful, younger, more clever, and in every way more attractive than Kathleen. I recognise these things clearly, but it does not appear, somehow, to alter the fact that I am in love with her. I think I have been in love with her all my life. We were boy and girl together, Margaret, and—and I give you my word," Kennaston cried, with his boyish flush, "I worship her! I simply cannot explain the perfectly unreasonable way in which I worship her!"

He was sincere. He loved Kathleen Saumarez as much as he was capable of loving any one—almost as much as he loved to dilate on his own peculiarities and emotions.

Margaret's gaze was intent upon him. "Yet," she marvelled, "you made love to me very tropically."

With unconcealed pride, Mr. Kennaston assented. "Didn't I?" he said. "I was in rather good form last night, I thought."

"And you were actually prepared to marry me?" she asked—"even after you knew I was poor?"

"I couldn't very well back out," he submitted, and then cocked his head on one side. "You see," he added, whimsically, "I was sufficiently a conceited ass to fancy you cared a little for me. So, of course, I was going to marry you and try to make you happy. But how dear—oh, how unutterably dear it was of you, Margaret, to decline to be made happy in any such fashion!" And Mr. Kennaston paused to chuckle and to regard her with genuine esteem and affection.

But still her candid eyes weighed him, and transparently found him wanting.

"You are thinking, perhaps, what an unutterable cad I have been?" he suggested.

"Yes—you are rather by way of being a cad, beautiful. But I can't help liking you, somehow. I dare say it's because you're honest with me. Nobody—nobody," Miss Hugonin lamented, a forlorn little quiver in her voice, "*ever* seemed to be honest with me except you, and now I know you weren't. Oh, beautiful, aren't I ever to have any real friends?" she pleaded, wistfully.

Kennaston had meant a deal to her, you see; he had been the one man she trusted. She had gloried in his fustian rhetoric, his glib artlessness, his airy scorn of money; and now all this proved mere pinchbeck. On a sudden, too, there woke in some bycorner of her heart a queasy realisation of how near she had come to loving Kennaston. The thought nauseated her.

"My dear," he answered, kindly, "you will have any number of friends now that you are poor. It was merely your money that kept you from having any. You see," Mr. Kennaston went on, with somewhat the air of one climbing upon his favourite hobby, "money is the only thing that counts nowadays. In America, the rich are necessarily our only aristocracy. It is quite natural. One cannot hope for an aristocracy of intellect, if only for the reason that not one person in a thousand has any; and birth does not count for much. Of course, it is quite true that all of our remote ancestors came over with William the Conqueror—I have sometimes thought that the number of steerage passengers his ships would accommodate must have been little short of marvellous— but it is equally true that the grandfathers of most of our leisure class were either deserving or dishonest persons—who either started life on a farm, and studied Euclid by the firelight and did all the other priggish things they thought would look well in a biography, or else met with marked success in embezzlement. So money, after all, is our only standard; and when a woman is as rich as you were yesterday she cannot hope for friends any more than the Queen of England can. You could have plenty of flatterers, toadies, sycophants—anything, in fine, but friends."

"I don't believe it," said Margaret, half angrily—"not a word of it. There *must* be some honest people in the world who don't consider that money is everything. You know there must be, beautiful!"

The poet laughed. "That," said he, affably, "is poppycock. You are repeating the sort of thing I said to you yesterday. I am honest now. The best of us, Margaret, cannot help being impressed by the power of money. It is the greatest power in the world, and we cannot—cannot possibly—look upon rich people as being quite like us. We must toady to them a bit, Margaret, whether we want to or not. The Eagle intimidates us all."

"I *hate* him!" Miss Hugonin announced, with vehemence.

Kennaston searched his pockets. After a moment he produced a dollar bill and showed her the Eagle on it.

"There," he said, gravely, "is the original of the Woods Eagle—the Eagle that intimidates us all. Do you remember what Shakespeare—one always harks back to Shakespeare to clinch an argument, because not even our foremost actors have been able to conceal the fact that he was, as somebody in Dickens acutely points out, 'a dayvilish clever fellow'— do you remember. I say, what Shakespeare observes as to this very Eagle?"

Miss Hugonin shook her little head till it glittered in the sunlight like a topaz. She cared no more for Shakespeare than the average woman does, and she was never quite comfortable when he was alluded to.

> *"He says," Mr. Kennaston quoted, solemnly:*
> *"The Eagle suffers little birds to sing,*
> *And is not careful what they mean thereby,*
> *Knowing that with the shadow of his wing*
> *He can at pleasure still their melody."*

"That's nonsense," said Margaret, calmly. "I haven't the *least* idea what you're talking about, and I don't believe you have either."

He waved the dollar bill with a heroical gesture. "Here," he asserted, "is the Eagle. And by the little birds, I have not a doubt he meant charity and independence and kindliness and truth and the rest of the standard virtues. That is quite as plausible as the interpretation of the average commentator. The presence of money chills these little birds—ah, it is lamentable, no doubt, but it is true."

"I don't believe it," said Margaret—quite as if that settled the question.

But now his hobby, rowelled by opposition, was spurred to loftier flights.

"Ah, the power of these great fortunes America has bred is monstrous," he suddenly cried. "And always they work for evil. If I were ever to write a melodrama, Margaret, I could wish for no more thorough-paced villain than a large fortune." Kennaston paused and laughed grimly. "We cringe to the Eagle!" said he. "Eh, well, why not? The Eagle is very powerful and very cruel. In the South yonder, the Eagle has penned over a million children in his factories, where day by day he drains the youth and health and very life out of their tired bodies; in sweat-shops, men and women are toiling for the Eagle, giving their lives for the pittance that he grudges them; in countless mines and mills, the Eagle is trading human lives for coal and flour; in Wall Street yonder, the Eagle is juggling as he will with life's necessities—thieving from the farmer, thieving from the consumer, thieving from the poor fools who try to play the Eagle's game, and driving them at will to despair and ruin and death: look whither you may, men die that the Eagle may grow fat. So the Eagle thrives, and daily the rich grow richer and the poor grow poorer, and the end——" Kennaston paused, staring into vacancy. "Eh, well," said he, with a smile and a snap of his fingers, "the end rests upon the knees of the gods. But there must need be an end some day. And meanwhile, you cannot blame us if we cringe to the Eagle that is master of the world. It is human nature to cringe to its master; and while human nature is not always an admirable thing, it is, I believe, rather widely distributed."

Margaret did not return the smile. Like any sensible woman, she never tolerated opinions that differed from her own.

So she waved his preachment aside. "You're trying to be eloquent," was her observation, "and you've only succeeded in being very silly and tiresome. Go away, beautiful. You make me awfully tired, and I don't care for you in the least. Go and talk to Kathleen. I shall be here—on this very spot," Margaret added, with commendable precision and an unaccountable increase of colour, "if—if any one should happen to ask."

Then Kennaston rose and laughed merrily.

"You are quite delicious," he commented. "It will always be a grief and a puzzle to me that I am not mad for love of you. It is unreasonable of me," he complained, sadly, and shook his head, "but I prefer Kathleen.

And I am quite certain that somebody will ask where you are. I shall describe to him the exact spot—"

Mr. Kennaston paused, with a slight air of apology.

"If I were you," he suggested, pleasantly, "I would move a little—just a little—to the left. That will enable you to obtain to a fuller extent the benefit of the sunbeam which is falling—quite by accident, of course—upon your hair. You are perfectly right, Margaret, in selecting that hedge as a background. Its sombre green sets you off to perfection."

He went away chuckling. He felt that Margaret must think him a devil of a fellow.

She didn't, though.

"The *idea* of his suspecting me of such unconscionable vanity!" she said, properly offended. Then, "Anyhow, a man has no business to know about such things," she continued, with rising indignation. "I believe Felix Kennaston is as good a judge of chiffons as any woman. That's effeminate, I think, and catty and absurd. I don't believe I ever liked him—not really, that is. Now, what would Billy care about sunbeams and backgrounds, I'd like to know! He'd never even notice them. Billy is a *man*. Why, that's just what father said yesterday!" Margaret cried, and afterward laughed happily. "I suppose old people are right sometimes—but, dear, dear, they're terribly unreasonable at others!"

Having thus uttered the ancient, undying plaint of youth, Miss Hugonin moved a matter of two inches to the left, and smiled, and waited contentedly. It was barely possible some one might come that way; and it is always a comfort to know that one is not exactly repulsive in appearance.

Also, there was the spring about her; and, chief of all, there was a queer fluttering in her heart that was yet not unpleasant. In fine, she was unreasonably happy for no reason at all.

I believe the foolish poets call this feeling love and swear it is divine; however, they will say anything for the sake of an ear-tickling jingle. And while it is true that scientists have any number of plausible and interesting explanations for this same feeling, I am sorry to say I have forgotten them.

I am compelled, then, to fall back upon those same unreliable, irresponsible rhymesters, and to insist with them that a maid waiting in the springtide for the man she loves is necessarily happy and very rarely puzzles her head over the scientific reason for it.

Chapter 21

B ut ten minutes later she saw Mr. Woods in the distance striding across the sunlit terraces, and was seized with a conviction that their interview was likely to prove a stormy one. There was an ominous stiffness in his gait.

"Oh, dear, dear!" Miss Hugonin wailed; "he's in a temper now, and he'll probably be just as disagreeable as it's possible for any one to be. I do wish men weren't so unreasonable! He looks exactly like a big, blue-eyed thunder-cloud just now—just now, when I'm sure he has every cause in the *world* to be very much pleased—after all I've done for him. He makes me awfully tired. I think he's *very ungrateful*. I—I think I'm rather afraid."

In fact, she was. Now that the meeting she had anticipated these twelve hours past was actually at hand, there woke in her breast an unreasoning panic. Miss Hugonin considered, and caught up her skirts, and whisked into the summer-house, and there sat down in the darkest corner and devoutly wished Mr. Woods in Crim Tartary, or Jericho, or, in a word, any region other than the gardens of Selwoode.

Billy came presently to the opening in the hedge and stared at the deserted bench. He was undeniably in a temper. But, then, how becoming it was! thought someone.

"Miss Hugonin!" he said, coldly.

Evidently (thought someone) he intends to be just as nasty as possible.

"Peggy!" said Mr. Woods, after a little.

Perhaps (thought someone) he won't be *very* nasty.

"Dear Peggy!" said Mr. Woods, in his most conciliatory tone.

Someone rearranged her hair complacently.

But there was no answer, save the irresponsible chattering of the birds, and with a sigh Billy turned upon his heel.

Then, by the oddest chance in the world, Margaret coughed.

I dare say it was damp in the summer-house; or perhaps it was caused by some passing bronchial irritation; or perhaps, incredible as it may seem, she coughed to show him where she was. But I scarcely think so, because Margaret insisted afterward—very positively, too— that she didn't cough at all.

Chapter 22

W ell!" Mr. Woods observed, lengthening the word somewhat.
In the intimate half-light of the summer-house, he loomed
prodigiously big. He was gazing downward in careful consideration of
three fat tortoise-shell pins and a surprising quantity of gold hair, which
was practically all that he could see of Miss Hugonin's person; for that
young lady had suddenly become a limp mass of abashed violet ruffles,
and had discovered new and irresistible attractions in the mosaics about
her feet.

Billy's arms were crossed on his breast and his right hand caressed
his chin meditatively. By and bye, "I wonder, now," he reflected, aloud,
"if you can give any reason—any possible reason—why you shouldn't be
locked up in the nearest sanatorium?"

"You needn't be rude, you know," a voice observed from the
neighbourhood of the ruffles, "because there isn't anything you can do
about it."

Mr. Woods ventured a series of inarticulate observations. "But
why?" he concluded, desperately. "But why, Peggy?—in Heaven's name,
what's the meaning of all this?"

She looked up. Billy was aware of two large blue stars; his heart
leapt; and then he recalled a pair of gray-green eyes that had regarded
him in much the same fashion not long ago, and he groaned.

"I was unfair to you last night," she said, and the ring of her odd, deep
voice, and the richness and sweetness of it, moved him to faint longing,
to a sick heart-hunger. It was tremulous, too, and very tender. "Yes, I was
unutterably unfair, Billy. You asked me to marry you when you thought
I was a beggar, and—and Uncle Fred *ought* to have left you the money.
It was on account of me that he didn't, you know. I really owed it to you.
And after the way I talked to you—so long as I had the money—I—and,
anyhow, its very disagreeable and eccentric and *horrid* of you to object to
being rich!" Margaret concluded, somewhat incoherently.

She had not thought it would be like this. He seemed so stern.

But, "Isn't that exactly like her?" Mr. Woods was demanding of his
soul. "She thinks she has been unfair to me—to me, whom she doesn't
care a button for, mind you. So she hands over a fortune to make up
for it, simply because that's the first means that comes to hand! Now,
isn't that perfectly unreasonable, and fantastic, and magnificent, and

incredible?—in short, isn't that Peggy all over? Why, God bless her, her heart's bigger than a barn-door! Oh, it's no wonder that fellow Kennaston was grinning just now when he sent me to her! He can afford to grin."

Aloud, he stated, "You're an angel, Peggy that's what you are. I've always suspected it, and I'm glad to know it now for a fact. But in this prosaic world not even angels are allowed to burn up wills for recreation. Why, bless my soul, child, you—why, there's no telling what trouble you might have gotten into!"

Miss Hugonin pouted. "You needn't be such a grandfather," she suggested, helpfully.

"But it's a serious business," he insisted. At this point Billy began to object to her pouting as distracting one's mind from the subject under discussion. "It—why, it's——"

"It's what?" she pouted, even more rebelliously.

"Crimson," said Mr. Woods, considering—"oh, the very deepest, duskiest crimson such as you can't get in tubes. It's a colour was never mixed on any palette. It's—eh? Oh, I beg your pardon."

"I think you ought to," said Margaret, primly. Nevertheless, she had brightened considerably.

"Of course," Mr. Woods continued with a fine colour, "I can't take the money. That's absurd."

"Is it?" she queried, idly. "Now, I wonder how you're going to help yourself?"

"Simplest thing in the world," he assured her. "You see this match, don't you, Peggy? Well, now you're going to give me that paper I see in that bag-thing at your waist, and I'm going to burn it till it's all nice, soft, feathery ashes that can't ever be probated. And then the first will, which is practically the same as the last, will be allowed to stand, and I'll tell your father all about the affair, because he ought to know, and you'll have to settle with those colleges. And in that way," Mr. Woods submitted, "Uncle Fred's last wishes will be carried out just as he expressed them, and there needn't be any trouble—none at all. So give me the will, Peggy?"

It is curious what a trivial matter love makes of felony.

Margaret's heart sank.

However, "Yes?" said she, encouragingly; "and what do you intend doing afterward?—"

"I—I shall probably live abroad," said Billy. "Cheaper, you know."

And here (he thought) was an excellent, an undreamed-of opportunity to inform her of his engagement. He had much better tell her now and have done. Mr. Woods opened his mouth and looked at Margaret, and closed it. Again she was pouting in a fashion that distracted one's mind.

"That would be most unattractive," said Miss Hugonin, calmly. "You're very stupid, Billy, to think of living abroad. Billy, I think you're almost as stupid as I am. I've been very stupid, Billy. I thought I liked Mr. Kennaston. I don't, Billy—not that way. I've just told him so. I'm not—I'm not engaged to anybody now, Billy. But wasn't it stupid of me to make such a mistake, Billy?"

That was a very interesting mosaic there in the summer-house.

"I don't understand," said Mr. Woods. His voice shook, and his hands lifted a little toward her and trembled.

Poor Billy dared not understand. Her eyes downcast, her foot tapping the floor gently, Margaret was all one blush. She, too, was trembling a little, and she was a little afraid and quite unutterably happy; and outwardly she was very much the tiny lady of Oberon's court, very much the coquette quintessentialised.

It is pitiable that our proud Margaret should come to such a pass. Ah, the men that you have flouted and scorned and bedeviled and mocked at, Margaret—could they see you now, I think the basest of them could not but pity and worship you. This man is bound in honour to another woman; yet a little, and his lips will open—very dry, parched lips they are now—and he will tell you, and your pride will drive you mad, and your heart come near to breaking.

"Don't you understand—oh, you silly Billy!" She was peeping at him meltingly from under her lashes.

"I—I'm imagining vain things," said Mr. Woods. "I—oh, Peggy, Peggy, I think I must be going mad!"

He stared hungrily at the pink, startled face that lifted toward his. Ah, no, no, it could not be possible, this thing he had imagined for a moment. He had misunderstood.

And now just for a little (thought poor Billy) let my eyes drink in those dear felicities of colour and curve, and meet just for a little the splendour of those eyes that have the April in them, and rest just for a little upon that sanguine, close-grained, petulant mouth; and then I will tell her, and then I think that I must die.

"Peggy——" he began, in a flattish voice.

"They have evidently gone," said the voice of Mr. Kennaston; "yes, those beautiful, happy young people have foolishly deserted the very prettiest spot in the gardens. Let us sit here, Kathleen."

"But I'm not an eavesdropper," Mr. Woods protested, half angrily.

I fear Margaret was not properly impressed.

"Please, Billy," she pleaded, in a shrill whisper, "please let's listen. He's going to propose to her now, and you've no idea how funny he is when he proposes. Oh, don't be so pokey, Billy—do let's listen!"

But Mr. Woods had risen with a strange celerity and was about to leave the summer-house.

Margaret pouted. Mrs. Saumarez and Mr. Kennaston were seated not twenty feet from the summer-house, on the bench which Miss Hugonin had just left. And when that unprincipled young woman finally rose to her feet, it must be confessed that it was with a toss of the head and with the reflection that while to listen wasn't honourable, it would at least be very amusing. I grieve to admit it, but with Billy's scruples she hadn't the slightest sympathy.

Then Kennaston cried, suddenly: "Why, you're mad, Kathleen! Woods wants to marry *you!* Why, he's heels over head in love with Miss Hugonin!"

Miss Hugonin turned to Mr. Woods with a little intake of the breath.

No, I shall not attempt to tell you what Billy saw in her countenance. Timanthes-like, I drape before it the vines of the summer-house. For a brief space I think we had best betake ourselves outside, leaving Margaret in a very pitiable state of anger, and shame, and humiliation, and heartbreak—leaving poor Billy with a heart that ached, seeing the horror of him in her face.

Chapter 23

Mrs. Saumarez laughed bitterly.

"No," she said, "Billy cared for me, you know, a long time ago. And this morning he told me he still cared. Billy doesn't pretend to be a clever man, you see, and so he can afford to practice some of the brute virtues, such as constancy and fidelity."

There was a challenging flame in her eyes, but Kennaston let the stab pass unnoticed. To do him justice, he was thinking less of himself, just now, than of how this news would affect Margaret; and his face was very grave and strangely tender, for in his own fashion he loved Margaret.

"It's nasty, very nasty," he said, at length, in a voice that was puzzled. "Yet I could have sworn yesterday——" Kennaston paused and laughed lightly. "She was an heiress yesterday, and to-day she is nobody. And Mr. Woods, being wealthy, can afford to gratify the virtues you commend so highly and, with a fidelity that is most edifying, return again to his old love. And she welcomes him—and the Woods millions—with open arms. It is quite affecting, is it not, Kathleen?"

"You needn't be disagreeable," she observed.

"My dear Kathleen, I assure you I am not angry. I am merely a little sorry for human nature. I could have sworn Woods was honest. But rogues all, rogues all, Kathleen! Money rules us in the end; and now the parable is fulfilled, and Love the prodigal returns to make merry over the calf of gold. Confess," Mr. Kennaston queried, with a smile, "is it not strange an all-wise Creator should have been at pains to fashion this brave world about us for little men and women such as we to lie and pilfer in? Was it worth while, think you, to arch the firmament above our rogueries, and light the ageless stars as candles to display our antics? Let us be frank, Kathleen, and confess that life is but a trivial farce ignobly played in a very stately temple." And Mr. Kennaston laughed again.

"Let us be frank!" Kathleen cried, with a little catch in her voice. "Why, it isn't in you to be frank, Felix Kennaston! Your life is nothing but a succession of poses—shallow, foolish poses meant to hoodwink the world and at times yourself. For you do hoodwink yourself, don't you, Felix?" she asked, eagerly, and gave him no time to answer. She feared, you see, lest his answer might dilapidate the one fortress she had been able to build about his honour.

"And now," she went on, quickly, "you're trying to make me think you a devil of a fellow, aren't you? And you're hinting that I've accepted Billy because of his money, aren't you? Well, it is true that I wouldn't marry him if he were poor. But he's very far from being poor. And he cares for me. And I am fond of him. And so I shall marry him and make him as good a wife as I can. So there!"

Mrs. Saumarez faced him with an uneasy defiance. He was smiling oddly.

"I have heard it rumoured in many foolish tales and jingling verses," said Kennaston, after a little, "that a thing called love exists in the world. And I have also heard, Kathleen, that it sometimes enters into the question of marriage. It appears that I was misinformed."

"No," she answered, slowly, "there is a thing called love. I think women are none the better for knowing it. To a woman, it means to take some man—some utterly commonplace man, perhaps—perhaps, only an idle *poseur* such as you are, Felix—and to set him up on a pedestal, and to bow down and worship him; and to protest loudly, both to the world and to herself, that in spite of all appearances her idol really hasn't feet of clay, or that, at any rate, it is the very nicest clay in the world. For a time she deceives herself, Felix. Then the idol topples from the pedestal and is broken, and she sees that it is all clay, Felix—clay through and through—and her heart breaks with it."

Kennaston bowed his head. "It is true," said he; "that is the love of women."

"To a man," she went on, dully, "it means to take some woman—the nearest woman who isn't actually deformed—and to make pretty speeches to her and to make her love him. And after a while—" Kathleen shrugged her shoulders drearily. "Why, after a while," said she, "he grows tired and looks for some other woman."

"It is true," said Kennaston—"yes, very true that some men love in that fashion."

There ensued a silence. It was a long silence, and under the tension of it Kathleen's composure snapped like a cord that has been stretched to the breaking point.

"Yes, yes, yes!" she cried, suddenly; "that is how I have loved you and that is how you've loved me, Felix Kennaston! Ah, Billy told me what happened last night! And that—that was why I—" Mrs. Saumarez paused and regarded him curiously. "You don't make a very noble figure, just now, do you?" she asked, with careful deliberation. "You were ready to sell yourself for Miss Hugonin's money, weren't you? And now you must take her without the money. Poor Felix! Ah, you poor, petty liar, who've over-reached yourself so utterly!" And again Kathleen began to laugh, but somewhat shrilly, somewhat hysterically.

"You are wrong," he said, with a flush. "It is true that I asked Miss Hugonin to marry me. But she—very wisely, I dare say—declined."

"Ah!" Kathleen said, slowly. Then—and it will not do to inquire too closely into her logic—she spoke with considerable sharpness: "She's a conceited little cat! I never in all my life knew a girl to be quite so conceited as she is. Positively, I don't believe she thinks there's a man breathing who's good enough for her!"

Kennaston grinned. "Oh, Kathleen, Kathleen!" he said; "you are simply delicious."

And Mrs. Saumarez coloured prettily and tried to look severe and could not, for the simple reason that, while she knew Kennaston to be flippant and weak and unstable as water and generally worthless, yet for some occult cause she loved him as tenderly as though he had been a paragon of all the manly virtues. And I dare say that for many of us it is by a very kindly provision of Nature that all women are created capable of doing this illogical thing and that most of them do it daily.

"It is true," the poet said, at length, "that I have played no heroic part. And I don't question, Kathleen, that I am all you think me. Yet, such as I am, I love you. And such as I am, you love me, and it is I that you are going to marry, and not that Woods person."

"He's worth ten of you!" she cried, scornfully.

"Twenty of me, perhaps," Mr. Kennaston assented, "but that isn't the question. You don't love him, Kathleen. You are about to marry him for his money. You are about to do what I thought to do yesterday. But you won't, Kathleen. You know that I need you, my dear, and—unreasonably enough, God knows—you love me."

Mrs. Saumarez regarded him intently for a considerable space, and during that space the Eagle warred in her heart with the one foe he can never conquer. Love had a worthless ally; but Love fought staunchly.

By and bye, "Yes," she said, and her voice was almost sullen; "I love you. I ought to love Billy, but I don't. I shall ask him to release me from my engagement. And yes, I will marry you if you like."

He raised her hand to his lips. "You are an angel," Mr. Kennaston was pleased to say.

"No," Mrs. Saumarez dissented, rather forlornly; "I'm simply a fool. Otherwise, I wouldn't be about to marry you, knowing you as I do for what you are—knowing that I haven't one chance in a hundred of any happiness."

"My dear," he said, and his voice was earnest, "you know at least that what there is of good in me is at its best with you."

"Yes, yes!" Kathleen cried, quickly. "That is so, isn't it, Felix? And you do care for me, don't you? Felix, are you sure you care for me—quite sure? And are you quite certain, Felix, that you never cared so much for any one else?"

Mr. Kennaston was quite certain. He proceeded to explain his feelings toward her at some length.

Kathleen listened with downcast eyes and almost cheated herself into the belief that the man she loved was all that he should be. But at the bottom of her heart she knew he wasn't.

I think we may fairly pity her.

Kennaston and Mrs. Saumarez chatted very amicably for some ten minutes. At the end of that period, the twelve forty-five express bellowing faintly in the distance recalled the fact that the morning mail was in, and thereupon, in the very best of humours, they set out for the house. I grieve to admit it, but Kathleen had utterly forgotten Billy by this, and was no more thinking of him than she was of the Man in the Iron Mask.

She was with Kennaston, you see; and her thoughts, and glances, and lips, and adoration were all given to his pleasuring, just as her life would have been if its loss could have saved him from a toothache. He strutted a little, and was a little grateful to her, and—to do him justice—received the tribute she accorded him with perfect satisfaction and equanimity.

Chapter 24

Margaret came out of the summer-house, Billy Woods followed her, in a very moist state of perturbation.

"Peggy——" said Mr. Woods.

But Miss Hugonin was laughing. Clear as a bird-call, she poured forth her rippling mimicry of mirth. They train women well in these matters. To Margaret, just now, her heart seemed dead within her. Her lover was proved unworthy. Her pride was shattered. She had loved this clumsy liar yonder, had given up a fortune for him, dared all for him, had (as the phrase runs) flung herself at his head. The shame of it was a physical sickness, a nausea. But now, in this jumble of miseries, in this breaking-up of the earth and the void heavens that surged about her and would not be mastered, the girl laughed; and her laughter was care-free and half-languid like that of a child who is thinking of something else. Ah, yes, they train women well in these matters.

At length Margaret said, in high, crisp accents: "Pardon me, but I can't help being amused, Mr. Woods, by the way in which hard luck dogs your footsteps. I think Fate must have some grudge against you, Mr. Woods."

"Peggy——" said Mr. Woods.

"Pardon me," she interrupted him, her masculine little chin high in the air, "but I wish you wouldn't call me that. It was well enough when we were boy and girl together, Mr. Woods. But you've developed since—ah, yes, you've developed into such a splendid actor, such a consummate liar, such a clever scoundrel, Mr. Woods, that I scarcely recognise you now."

And there was not a spark of anger in the very darkest corner of Billy's big, brave heart, but only pity—pity all through and through, that sent little icy ticklings up and down his spine and turned his breathing to great sobs. For she had turned full face to him and he could see the look in her eyes.

I think he has never forgotten it. Years after the memory of it would come upon him suddenly and set hot drenching waves of shame and remorse surging about his body—remorse unutterable that he ever hurt his Peggy so deeply. For they were tragic eyes. Beneath them her twitching mouth smiled bravely, but the mirth of her eyes was monstrous. It was the mirth of a beaten woman, of a woman who has known the last extreme of shame and misery and has learned to laugh at it. Even now Billy Woods cannot quite forget.

"Peggy," said he, brokenly, "ah, dear, dear Peggy, listen to me!"

"Why, have you thought of a plausible lie so soon?" she queried, sweetly. "Dear me, Mr. Woods, what is the use of explaining things? It is very simple. You wanted to marry me last night because I was rich. And when I declined the honour, you went back to your old love. Oh, it's very simple, Mr. Woods! It's a pity, though—isn't it?—that all your promptness went for nothing. Why, dear me, you actually managed to propose before breakfast, didn't you? I should have thought that such eagerness would have made an impression on Kathleen—oh, a most favourable impression. Too bad it hasn't!"

"Listen!" said Billy. "Ah, you're forcing me to talk like a cad, Peggy, but I can't see you suffer—I can't! Kathleen misunderstood what I said to her. I—I didn't mean to propose to her, Peggy. It was a mistake, I tell you. It's you I love—just you. And when I asked you to marry me last night—why, I thought the money was mine, Peggy. I'd never have asked you if I hadn't thought that. I—ah, you don't believe me, you don't believe me, Peggy, and before God, I'm telling you the simple truth! Why, I hadn't ever seen that last will, Peggy! It was locked up in that centre place in the desk, you remember. Why—why, you yourself had the keys to it, Peggy. Surely, you remember, dear?" And Billy's voice shook and skipped whole octaves as he pleaded with her, for he knew she did not believe him and he could not endure the horror of her eyes.

But Margaret shook her head; and as aforetime the twitching lips continued to laugh beneath those tragic eyes. Ah, poor little lady of Elfland! poor little Undine, with a soul wakened to suffering!

"Clumsy, very clumsy!" she rebuked him. "I see that you are accustomed to prepare your lies in advance, Mr. Woods. As an extemporaneous liar you are very clumsy. Men don't propose by mistake except in farces. And while we are speaking of farces, don't you think it time to drop that one of your not knowing about that last will?"

"The farce!" Billy stammered. "You—why, you saw me when I found it!"

"Ah, yes, I saw you when you pretended to find it. I saw you when you pretended to unlock that centre place. But now, of course, I know it never was locked. I'm very careless about locking things, Mr. Woods. Ah, yes, that gave you a beautiful opportunity, didn't it? So, when you were rummaging through my desk—without my permission, by the way, but that's a detail—you found both wills and concocted your little comedy? That was very clever. Oh, you think you're awfully smooth, don't you, Billy Woods? But if you had been a bit more daring, don't you see, you could have suppressed the last one and taken the money without being encumbered by me? That was rather clumsy of you, wasn't it?" Suave, gentle, sweet as honey was the speech of Margaret as she lifted her face to his, but her eyes were tragedies.

"Ah!" said Billy. "Ah—yes—you think—that." He was very careful in articulating his words, was Billy, and afterward he nodded his head gravely. The universe had somehow suffered an airy dissolution like that of Prospero's masque—Selwoode and its gardens, the great globe itself, "the cloud-capped towers, the gorgeous palaces, the solemn temples" were all as vanished wraiths. There was only Peggy left—Peggy with that unimaginable misery in her eyes that he must drive away somehow. If that was what she thought, there was no way for him to prove it wasn't so.

"Why, dear me, Mr. Woods," she retorted, carelessly, "what else could I think?"

Here Mr. Woods blundered.

"Ah, think what you will, Peggy!" he cried, his big voice cracking and sobbing and resonant with pain. "Ah, my dear, think what you will, but don't grieve for it, Peggy! Why, if I'm all you say I am, that's no reason you should suffer for it! Ah, don't, Peggy! In God's name, don't! I can't bear it, dear," he pleaded with her, helplessly.

Billy was suffering, too. But her sorrow was the chief of his, and what stung him now to impotent anger was that she must suffer and he be unable to help her—for, ah, how willingly, how gladly, he would have borne all poor Peggy's woes upon his own broad shoulders.

But none the less, he had lost an invaluable opportunity to hold his tongue.

"Suffer! I suffer!" she mocked him, languidly; and then, like a banjo-string, the tension snapped, and she gave a long, angry gasp, and her wrath flamed.

"Upon my word, you're the most conceited man I ever knew in my life! You think I'm in love with you! With you! Billy Woods, I wouldn't wipe my feet on you if you were the last man left on earth! I hate you, I loathe you, I detest you, I despise you! Do you hear me?—I hate you. What do I care if you *are* a snob, and a cad, and a fortune-hunter, and a forger, and—well, I don't care! Perhaps you haven't ever forged anything yet, but I'm quite sure you would if you ever got an opportunity. You'd be delighted to do it. Yes, you would—you're just the sort of man who *revels* in crime. I love you! Why, that's the best joke I've heard for a long time. I'm only sorry for you, Billy Woods—*sorry* because Kathleen has thrown you over—sorry, do you understand? Yes, since you're so fond of skinny women, I think it's a great pity she wouldn't have you. Don't talk to me!—she *is* skinny. I guess I know. She's as skinny as a beanpole. She's skinnier than I ever imagined it possible for anybody—*anybody*—to be. And she pads and rouges till I think it's disgusting, and not half—not *one-half*—of her hair belongs to her, and that half is dyed. But, of course, if you like that sort of thing, there's no accounting for tastes, and I'm sure I'm very sorry for you, even though personally I *don't* care for skinny women. I hate 'em! And I hate you, too, Billy Woods!"

She stamped her foot, did Margaret. You must bear with her, for her heart is breaking now, and if she has become a termagant it is because her shamed pride has driven her mad. Bear with her, then, a little longer.

Billy tried to bear with her, for in part he understood.

"Peggy," said he, very gently, "you're wrong."

"Yes, I dare say!" she snapped at him.

"We won't discuss Kathleen, if you please. But you're wrong about the will. I've told you the whole truth about that, but I don't blame you for not believing me, Peggy—ah, no, not I. There seems to be a curse upon Uncle Fred's money. It brings out the worst of all of us. It has changed even you, Peggy—and not for the better, Peggy. You've become distrustful. You—ah, well, we won't discuss that now. Give me the will, my dear, and I'll burn it before your eyes. That ought to show you, Peggy, that you're wrong." Billy was very white-lipped as he ended, for the Woods temper is a short one.

But she had an arrow left for him. "Give it to you! And do you think I'd trust you with it, Billy Woods?"

"Peggy!—ah, Peggy, I hadn't deserved that. Be just, at least, to me," poor Billy begged of her.

Which was an absurd thing to ask of an angry woman.

"Yes, I *do* know what you'd do with it! You'd take it right off and have it probated or executed or whatever it is they do to wills, and turn me straight out in the gutter. That's just what you're *longing* to do this very moment. Oh, I know, Billy Woods—I know what a temper you've got, and I know you're keeping quiet now simply because you know that's the most exasperating thing you can possibly do. I wouldn't have such a disposition as you've got for the world. You've absolutely *no* control over your temper—not a bit of it. You're *vile*, Billy Woods! Oh, I *hate* you!

Yes, you've made me cry, and I suppose you're very proud of yourself. *Aren't* you proud? Don't stand staring at me like a stuck pig, but answer me when I talk to you! Aren't you *proud* of making me cry? Aren't you? Ah, don't talk to me—don't talk to *me*, I tell you! I don't wish to hear a word you've got to say. I *hate* you. And you shan't have the money, that's flat."

"I don't want it," said Billy. "I've been trying to tell you for the last, half-hour I don't want it. In God's name, why can't you talk like a sensible woman, Peggy?" I am afraid that Mr. Woods, too, was beginning to lose his temper.

"That's right—swear at me! It only needed that. You do want the money, and when you say you don't you're lying—lying—*lying*, do you understand? You all want my money. Oh, dear, *dear!*" Margaret wailed, and her great voice was shaken to its depths and its sobbing was the long, hopeless sobbing of a violin, as she flung back her tear-stained face, and clenched her little hands tight at her sides; "why *can't* you let me alone? You're all after my money—you, and Mr. Kennaston, and Mr. Jukesbury, and all of you! Why *can't* you let me alone? Ever since I've had it you've hunted me as if I'd been a wild beast. God help me, I haven't had a moment's peace, a moment's rest, a, moment's quiet, since Uncle Fred died. They all want my money—everybody wants my money! Oh, Billy, Billy, why *can't* they let me alone?"

"Peggy——" said he.

But she interrupted him. "Don't talk to *me*, Billy Woods! Don't you *dare* talk to me. I told you I didn't wish to hear a word you had to say, didn't I? Yes, you all want my money. And you shan't have it. It's mine. Uncle Fred left it to me. It's mine, I tell you. I've got the greatest thing in the world—money! And I'll keep it. Ah, I hate you all—every one of you—but I'll make you cringe to me. I'll make you *all* cringe, do you hear, because I've got the money you're ready to sell your paltry souls for! Oh, I'll make you cringe most of all, Billy Woods! I'm rich, do you hear?—rich—*rich*! Wouldn't you be glad to marry the rich Margaret Hugonin, Billy? Ah, haven't you schemed hard for that? You'd be glad to do it, wouldn't you? You'd give your dirty little soul for that, wouldn't you, Billy? Ah, what a cur you are! Well, some day perhaps I'll buy you just as I would any other cur. Wouldn't you be glad if I did, Billy? Beg for it, Billy! Beg, sir! Beg!" And Margaret flung back her head again, and laughed shrilly, and held up her hand before him as one holds a lump of sugar before a pug-dog.

In Selwoode I can fancy how the Eagle screamed his triumph.

But Billy's face was ashen.

"Before God!" he said, between his teeth, "loving you as I do, I wouldn't marry you now for all the wealth in the world! The money has ruined you—ruined you, Peggy."

For a little she stared at him. By and bye, "I dare say it has," she said, in a strangely sober tone. "I've been scolding like a fishwife. I beg your pardon, Mr. Woods—not for what I've said, because I meant every *word* of it, but I beg your pardon for saying it. Don't come with me, please."

Blindly she turned from him. Her shoulders had the droop of an old woman's. Margaret was wearied now, weary with the weariness of death.

For a while Mr. Woods stared after the tired little figure that trudged straight onward in the sunlight, stumbling as she went. Then a pleached walk swallowed her, and Mr. Woods groaned.

"Oh, Peggy, Peggy!" he said, in bottomless compassion; "oh, my poor little Peggy! How changed you are!"

Afterward Mr. Woods sank down upon the bench and buried his face in his hands. He sat there for a long time. I don't believe he thought of anything very clearly. His mind was a turgid chaos of misery; and about him the birds shrilled and quavered and carolled till the air was vibrant with their trilling. One might have thought they choired in honour of the Eagle's triumph, in mockery of poor Billy.

Then Mr. Woods raised his head with a queer, alert look. Surely he had heard a voice—the dearest of all voices.

"Billy!" it wailed; "oh, Billy, *Billy*!"

Chapter 25

For at the height of this particularly mischancy posture of affairs the meddlesome Fates had elected to dispatch Cock-eye Flinks to serve as our *deus ex machina*. And just as in the comedy the police turn up in the nick of time to fetch Tartuffe to prison, or in the tragedy Friar John manages to be detained on his journey to Mantua and thus bring about that lamentable business in the tomb of the Capulets, so Mr. Flinks now happens inopportunely to arrive upon our lesser stage.

Faithfully to narrate how Cock-eye Flinks chanced to be at Selwoode were a task of magnitude. That gentleman travelled very quietly; and for the most part, he journeyed incognito under a variety of aliases suggested partly by a fertile imagination and in part by prudential motives. For his notions of proprietary rights were deplorably vague, and his acquaintance with the police, in consequence, extensive. And finally, that he was now at Selwoode was not in the least his fault, but all the doing of an N. & O. brakesman, who had in uncultured argument, reinforced by a coupling-pin, persuaded Mr. Flinks to disembark from the northern freight on the night previous.

Mr. Flinks, then, sat leaning against a tree in the gardens of Selwoode, some thirty feet from the wall that stands between Selwoode and Gridlington, and nursed his pride and foot, both injured in that high debate of last evening, and with a jackknife rounded off the top of a substantial staff designed to alleviate his present lameness. Meanwhile, he tempered his solitude with music, whistling melodiously the air of a song that pertained to the sacredness of home and of a white-haired mother.

Subsequently to Cock-eye Flinks (as the playbill has it), enter a vision in violet ruffles.

Wide-eyed, she came upon him in her misery, steadily trudging toward an unknown goal. I think he startled her a bit. Indeed, it must be admitted that Mr. Flinks, while a man of undoubted talent in his particular line of business, was, like many of your great geniuses, in outward aspect unprepossessing and misleading; for whereas he looked like a very shiftless and very dirty tramp, he was as a matter of fact as vile a rascal as ever pawned a swinish soul for whiskey.

"What are you doing here?" said Margaret, sharply. "Don't you know this is private property?"

To his feet rose Cock-eye Flinks. "Lady," said he, with humbleness, "you wouldn't be hard on a poor workingman, would you? It ain't my fault I'm here, lady—at least, it ain't rightly my fault. I just climbed over the wall to rest a minute—just a minute, lady, in the shade of these beautiful trees. I ain't a-hurting nobody by that, lady, I hope."

"Well, you had no business to do it," Miss Hugonin pointed out, "and you can just climb right back." Then she regarded him more intently, and her face softened somewhat. "What's the matter with your foot?" she demanded.

"Brakesman," said Mr. Flinks, briefly. "Threw me off a train. He struck me cruel hard, he did, and me a poor workingman trying to make my way to New York, lady, where my poor old mother's dying, lady, and me out of a job. Ah, it's a hard, hard world, lady—and me her only son—and he struck me cruel, cruel hard, he did, but I forgive him for it, lady. Ah, lady, you're so beautiful I know you're got a kind, good heart, lady. Can't you do something for a poor workingman, lady, with a poor dying mother—and a poor, sick wife," Mr. Flinks added as a dolorous afterthought; and drew nearer to her and held out one hand appealingly.

Petheridge Jukesbury had at divers times pointed out to her the evils of promiscuous charity, and these dicta Margaret parroted glibly enough, to do her justice, so long as there was no immediate question of dispensing alms. But for all that the next whining beggar would move her tender heart, his glib inventions playing upon it like a fiddle, and she would give as recklessly as though there were no such things in the whole wide world as soup-kitchens and organised charities and common-sense. "Because, you know," she would afterward salve her conscience, "I *couldn't* be sure he didn't need it, whereas I was *quite* sure I didn't."

Now she wavered for a moment. "You didn't say you had a wife before," she suggested.

"An invalid," sighed Mr. Flinks—"a helpless invalid, lady. And six small children probably crying for bread at this very moment. Ah, lady, think what my feelings must be to hear 'em cry in vain—think what I must suffer to know that I summoned them cherubs out of Heaven into this here hard, hard world, lady, and now can't do by 'em properly!" And Cock-eye Flinks brushed away a tear which I, for one, am inclined to regard as a particularly ambitious flight of his imagination.

Promptly Margaret opened the bag at her waist and took out her purse. "Don't!" she pleaded. "Please don't! I—I'm upset already. Take this, and please—oh, *please*, don't spend it in getting drunk or gambling or anything horrid," Miss Hugonin implored him. "You all do, and it's so selfish of you and so discouraging."

Mr. Flinks eyed the purse hungrily. Such a fat purse! thought Cock-eye Plinks. And there ain't nobody within a mile of here, neither. You are not to imagine that Mr. Flinks was totally abandoned; his vices were parochial, restrained for the most part by a lively apprehension of the law. But now the spell of the Eagle was strong upon him.

"Lady," said Mr. Flinks, twisting in his grimy hand the bill she had given him—and there, too, the Eagle flaunted in his vigour and heartened him, "lady, that ain't much for you to give. Can't you do a little better than that by a poor workingman, lady?"

A very unpleasant-looking person, Mr. Cock-eye Flinks. Oh, a peculiarly unpleasant-looking person to be a model son and a loving husband and a tender father. Margaret was filled with a vague alarm.

But she was brave, was Margaret. "No," said she, very decidedly, "I shan't give you another cent. So you climb right over that wall and go straight back where you belong."

The methods of Mr. Flinks, I regret to say, were somewhat more crude than those of Mesdames Haggage and Saumarez and Messieurs Kennaston and Jukesbury.

"Cheese it!" said Mr. Flinks, and flung away his staff and drew very near to her. "Gimme that money, do you hear!"

"Don't you dare touch me!" she panted; "ah, don't you *dare*!"

"Aw, hell!" said Mr. Flinks, disgustedly, and his dirty hands were upon her, and his foul breath reeked in her face.

In her hour of need Margaret's heart spoke.

"Billy!" she wailed; "oh, Billy, *Billy*!"

HE CAME TO HER—JUST as he would have scaled Heaven to come to her, just as he would have come to her in the nethermost pit of Hell if she had called. Ah, yes, Billy Woods came to her now in her peril, and I don't think that Mr. Flinks particularly relished the look upon Billy's face as he ran through the gardens, for Billy was furiously moved.

Cock-eye Flinks glanced back at the wall behind him. Ten feet high, and the fellow ain't far off. Cock-eye Flinks caught up his staff, and as Billy closed upon him, struck him full on the head. Again and again he struck him. It was a sickening business.

Billy had stopped short. For an instant he stood swaying on his feet, a puzzled face showing under the trickling blood. Then he flung out his hands a little, and they flapped loosely at the wrists, like wet clothes hung in the wind to dry, and Billy seemed to crumple up suddenly, and slid down upon the grass in an untidy heap.

"Ah-h-h!" said Mr. Flinks. He drew back and stared stupidly at that sprawling flesh which just now had been a man, and was seized with uncontrollable shuddering. "Ah-h-h!" said Mr. Flinks, very quietly.

And Margaret went mad. The earth and the sky dissolved in many floating specks and then went red—red like that heap yonder. The veneer of civilisation peeled, fell from her like snow from a shaken garment. The primal beast woke and flicked aside the centuries' work. She was the Cave-woman who had seen the death of her mate—the brute who had been robbed of her mate.

"Damn you! *Damn* you!" she screamed, her voice high, flat, quite unhuman; "ah, God in Heaven damn you!" With inarticulate bestial cries she fell upon the man who had killed Billy, and her violet fripperies fluttered, her impotent little hands beat at him, tore at him. She was fearless, shameless, insane. She only knew that Billy was dead.

With an oath the man flung her from him and turned on his heel. She fell to coaxing the heap in the grass to tell her that he forgave her— to open his eyes—to stop bloodying her dress—to come to luncheon. . .

A fly settled on Billy's face and came in his zig-zag course to the red stream trickling from his nostrils, and stopped short. She brushed the carrion thing away, but it crawled back drunkenly. She touched it with her finger, and the fly would not move. On a sudden, every nerve in her body began to shake and jerk like a flag snapping in the wind.

Chapter 26

Some ten minutes afterward, as the members of the house-party sat chatting on the terrace before Selwoode, there came among them a mad woman in violet trappings that were splotched with blood.

"Did you know that Billy was dead?" she queried, smilingly. "Oh, yes, a man killed Billy just now. Wasn't it too bad? Billy was such a nice boy, you know. I—I think it's very sad. I think it's the saddest thing I ever knew of in my life."

Kathleen Saumarez was the first to reach her. But she drew back quickly.

"No, ah, no!" she said, with a little shudder. "You didn't love Billy. He loved you, and you didn't love him. Oh, Kathleen, Kathleen, how *could* you help loving Billy? He was such a nice boy. I—I'm rather sorry he's dead."

Then she stood silent, picking at her dress thoughtfully and still smiling. Afterward, for the first and only time in history, Miss Hugonin fainted—fainted with an anxious smile.

Petheridge Jukesbury caught her as she fell, and began to blubber like a whipped schoolboy as he stood there holding her in his arms.

Chapter 27

B ut Billy was not dead. There was still a feeble, jerky fluttering in his big chest when Colonel Hugonin found him. His heart still moved, but under the Colonel's hand its stirrings were vague and aimless as those of a captive butterfly.

The Colonel had seen dead men and dying men before this; and as he bent over the boy he loved he gave a convulsive sob, and afterward buried his face in his hands.

Then—of all unlikely persons in the world—it was Petheridge Jukesbury who rose to meet the occasion.

His suavity and blandness forgotten in the presence of death, he mounted with confident alacrity to heights of greatness. Masterfully, he overrode them all. He poured brandy between Billy's teeth. Then he ordered the ladies off to bed, and recommended to Mr. Kennaston— when that gentleman spoke of a clergyman—a far more startling destination.

For, "It is far from my intention," said Mr.

Jukesbury, "to appear lacking in respect to the cloth, but—er—just at present I am inclined to think we are in somewhat greater need of a mattress and a doctor and—ah—the exercise of a little common-sense. The gentleman is—er—let us hope, in no immediate danger."

"How dare you suggest such a thing, sir?" thundered Petheridge Jukesbury. "Didn't you see that poor girl's face? I tell you I'll be damned if he dies, sir!"

And I fancy the recording angel heard him, and against a list of wordy cheats registered that oath to his credit.

It was Petheridge Jukesbury, then, who stalked into Mrs. Haggage's apartments and appropriated her mattress as the first at hand, and afterward waddled through the gardens bearing it on his fat shoulders, and still later lifted Billy upon it as gently as a woman could have. But it was the hatless Colonel on his favourite Black Bess ("Damn your motor-cars!" the Colonel was wont to say; "I consider my appearance sufficiently unprepossessing already, sir, without my arriving in Heaven in fragments and stinking of gasoline!") who in Fairhaven town, some quarter of an hour afterward, leaped Dr. Jeal's garden fence, and subsequently bundled the doctor into his gig; and again yet later it was the Colonel who stood fuming upon the terrace with Dr. Jeal on his way to Selwoode indeed, but still some four miles from the mansion toward which he was urging his staid horse at its liveliest gait.

Kennaston tried to soothe him. But the Colonel clamoured to the heavens. Kennaston he qualified in various ways. And as for Dr. Jeal, he would hold him responsible—"personally, sir"—for the consequences of his dawdling in this fashion—"Damme, sir, like a damn' snail with a wooden leg!"

"I am afraid," said Kennaston, gravely, "that the doctor will be of very little use when he does arrive."

There was that in his face which made the Colonel pause in his objurgations.

"Sir," said the Colonel, "what—do—you—mean?" He found articulation somewhat difficult.

"In your absence," Kennaston answered, "Mr. Jukesbury, who it appears knows something of medicine, has subjected Mr. Woods to an examination. It—it would be unkind to deceive you——"

"Come to the point, sir," the Colonel interrupted him. "What—do you—mean?"

"I mean," said Felix Kennaston, sadly, "that—he is afraid—Mr. Woods will never recover consciousness."

Colonel Hugonin stared at him. The skin of his flabby, wrinkled old throat was working convulsively.

Then, "You're wrong, sir," the Colonel said. "Billy *shan't* die. Damn Jukesbury! Damn all doctors, too, sir! I put my trust in my God, sir, and not in a box of damn' sugar-pills, sir. And I tell you, sir, *that boy is not going to die*."

Afterward he turned and went into Selwoode defiantly.

Chapter 28

I n the living-hall the Colonel found Margaret, white as paper, with purple lips that timidly smiled at him.

"Why ain't you in bed?" the old gentleman demanded, with as great an affectation of sternness as he could muster. To say the truth, it was not much; for Colonel Hugonin, for all his blustering optimism, was sadly shaken now.

"Attractive," said Margaret, "I was, but I couldn't stay there. My—my brain won't stop working, you see," she complained, wearily. "There's a thin little whisper in the back of it that keeps telling me about Billy, and what a liar he is, and what nice eyes he has, and how poor Billy is dead. It keeps telling me that, over and over again, attractive. It's such a tiresome, silly little whisper. But he is dead, isn't he? Didn't Mr. Kennaston tell me just now that he was dead?—or was it the whisper, attractive?"

The Colonel coughed. "Kennaston—er—Kennaston's a fool," he declared, helplessly. "Always said he was a fool. We'll have Jeal in presently."

"No—I remember now—Mr. Kennaston said Billy would die very soon. You don't like people to disagree with you, do you, attractive? Of course, he will die, for the man hit him very, *very* hard. I'm sorry Billy is going to die, though, even if he is such a liar!"

"Don't!" said the Colonel, hoarsely; "don't, daughter! I don't know what there is between you and Billy, but you're wrong. Oh, you're very hopelessly wrong! Billy's the finest boy I know."

Margaret shook her head in dissent.

"No, he's a very contemptible liar," she said, disinterestedly, "and that is what makes it so queer that I should care for him more than I do for anything else in the world. Yes, it's very queer."

Then Margaret went into the room opening into the living-hall, where Billy Woods lay unconscious, pallid, breathing stertorously. And the Colonel stared after her.

"Oh, my God, my God!" groaned the poor Colonel; "why couldn't it have been I? Why couldn't it have been I that ain't wanted any longer? She'd never have grieved like that for me!"

And indeed, I don't think she would have.

For to Margaret there had come, as, God willing, there comes to every clean-souled woman, the time to put away all childish things, and all childish memories, and all childish ties, if need be, to follow one man only, and cleave to him, and know his life and hers to be knit up together, past severance, in a love that death itself may not affright nor slay.

Chapter 29

S he sat silent in one corner of the darkened room. It was the bedroom that Frederick R. Woods formerly occupied—on the ground floor of Selwoode, opening into the living-hall—to which they had carried Billy.

Jukesbury had done what he could. In the bed lay Billy Woods, swathed in hot blankets, with bottles of hot water set to his feet. Jukesbury had washed his face clean of that awful red, and had wrapped bandages of cracked ice about his head and propped it high with pillows. It was little short of marvellous to see the pursy old hypocrite going cat-footed about the room on his stealthy ministrations, replenishing the bandages, forcing spirits of ammonia between Billy's teeth, fighting deftly and confidently with death.

Billy still breathed.

The Colonel came and went uneasily. The clock on the mantel ticked. Margaret brooded in a silence that was only accentuated by that horrible wheezing, gurgling, tremulous breathing in the bed yonder. Would the doctor never come!

She was curiously conscious of her absolute lack of emotion.

But always the interminable thin whispering in the back of her head went on and on. "Oh, if he had only died four years ago! Oh, if he had only died the dear, clean-minded, honest boy I used to know! When that noise stops he will be dead. And then, perhaps, I shall be able to cry. Oh, if he had only died four years ago!"

And then *da capo*. On and on ran the interminable thin whispering as Margaret waited for death to come to Billy. Billy looked so old now, under his many bandages. Surely he must be very, very near death.

Suddenly, as Jukesbury wrapped new bandages about his forehead, Billy opened his eyes and, without further movement, smiled placidly up at him.

"Hello, Jukesbury," said Billy Woods, "where's my armour?"

Jukesbury, too, smiled. "The man is bringing it downstairs now," he answered, quietly.

"Because," Billy went on, fretfully, "I don't propose to miss the Trojan war. The princes orgulous with high blood chafed, you know, are all going to be there, and I don't propose to miss it."

Behind his fat back, Petheridge Jukesbury waved a cautioning hand at Margaret, who had risen from her chair.

"But it is very absurd," Billy murmured, in the mere ghost of a voice, "because men don't propose by mistake except in farces. Somebody told me that, but I can't remember who, because I am a misogynist. That is a Greek word, and I would explain it to Peggy, if she would only give me a chance, but she can't because she has those seventeen hundred and fifty thousand children to look after. There must be some way to explain to her, though, because where there's a will there is always a way, and there were three wills. Uncle Fred should not have left so many wills—who would have thought the old man had so much ink in him? But I will be a very great painter, Uncle Fred, and make her sorry for the way she has treated me, and *then* Kathleen will understand I was talking about Peggy."

His voice died away, and Margaret sat with wide eyes listening for it again. Would the doctor never come!

Billy was smiling and picking at the sheets.

"But Peggy is so rich," the faint voice presently complained—"so beastly rich! There is gold in her hair, and if you will look very closely you will see that her lashes were pure gold until she dipped them in the ink-pot. Besides, she expects me to sit up and beg for lumps of sugar, and I *never* take sugar in my coffee. And Peggy doesn't drink coffee at all, so I think it is very unfair, especially as Teddy Anstruther drinks like a fish and she is going to marry him. Peggy, why won't you marry me? You know I've always loved you, Peggy, and now I can tell you so because Uncle Fred has left me all his money. You think a great deal about money, Peggy. You said it was the greatest thing in the world. And it must be, because it is the only thing—the *only* thing, Peggy—that has been strong enough to keep us apart. A part is never greater than the whole, Peggy, but I will explain about that when you open that desk. There are sharks in it. Aren't there, Peggy?—*aren't* there?"

His voice had risen to a querulous tone. Gently the fat old man restrained him.

"Yes," said Petheridge Jukesbury; "dear me, yes. Why, dear me, of course."

But his warning hand held Margaret back—Margaret, who stood with big tears trickling down her cheeks.

"Dearer than life itself," Billy assented, wearily, "but before God, loving you as I do, I wouldn't marry you now for all the wealth in the world. I forget why, but all the world is a stage, you know, and they don't use stages now, but only railroads. Is that why you rail at me so,

JAMES BRANCH CABELL

Peggy? That is a joke. You ought to laugh at my jokes, because I love you, but I can't ever, ever tell you so because you are rich. A rich man cannot pass through a needle's eye. Oh, Peggy, Peggy, I love your eyes, but they're so *big*, Peggy!"

So Billy Woods lay still and babbled ceaselessly. But through all his irrelevant talk, as you may see a tributary stream pulse unsullied in a muddied river, ran the thought of Peggy—of Peggy, and of her cruelty, and of her beauty, and of the money that stood between them.

And Margaret, who could never have believed him in his senses, listened and knew that in his delirium, the rudder of his thoughts snapped, he could not but speak truth. As she crouched in the corner of the room, her face buried in an arm-chair, her gold hair half loosened, her shoulders monotonously heaving, she wept gently, inaudibly, almost happily.

Almost happily. Billy was dying, but she knew now, past any doubting, that he loved her. The dear, clean-minded, honest boy had come back to her, and she could love him now without shame, and there was only herself to be loathed.

Then the door opened. Then, with Colonel Hugonin, came Martin Jeal—a wisp of a man like a November leaf—and regarded them from under his shaggy white hair with alert eyes.

"Hey, what's this?" said Dr. Jeal. "Eh, yes! Eh—yes!" he meditated, slowly. "Most irregular. You must let us have the room, Miss Hugonin."

In the hall she waited. Hope! ah, of course, there was no hope! the thin little whisper told her.

By and bye, though—after centuries of waiting—the three men came into the hall.

"Miss Hugonin," said Dr. Jeal, with a strange kindness in his voice, "I don't think we shall need you again. I am happy to tell you, though, that the patient is doing nicely—very nicely indeed."

Margaret clutched his arm. "You—you mean——"

"I mean," said Dr. Jeal, "that there is no fracture. A slight concussion of the brain, madam, and—so far as I can see—no signs of inflammation. Barring accidents, I think we'll have that young man out of bed in a week. Thanks," he added, "to Mr.—er—Jukesbury here whose prompt action was, under Heaven, undoubtedly the means of staving off meningitis and probably—indeed, more than probably—the means of saving Mr. Woods's life. It was splendid, sir, splendid! No doctor—why, God bless my soul!"

For Miss Hugonin had thrown her arms about Petheridge Jukesbury's neck and had kissed him vigorously.

"You beautiful child!" said Miss Hugonin.

"Er—Jukesbury," said the Colonel, mysteriously, "there's a little cognac in the cellar that—er—" The Colonel jerked his thumb across the hallway with the air of a conspirator. "Eh?" said the Colonel.

"Why—er—yes," said Mr. Jukesbury. "Why—ah—yes, I think I might."

They went across the hall together. The Colonel's hand rested fraternally on Petheridge Jukesbury's shoulder.

Chapter 30

The next day there was a general exodus from Selwoode, and Margaret's satellites dispersed upon their divers ways. Selwoode, as they understood it, was no longer hers; and they knew Billy Woods well enough to recognise that from Selwoode's new master there were no desirable pickings to be had such as the philanthropic crew had fattened on these four years past. So there came to them, one and all, urgent telegrams or insistent letters or some equally unanswerable demand for their presence elsewhere, such as are usually prevalent among our guests in very dull or very troublous times.

Miss Hugonin smiled a little bitterly. She considered that the scales had fallen from her eyes, and flattered herself that she was by way of becoming a bit of a misanthrope; also, I believe, there was a note concerning the hollowness of life and the worthlessness of society in general. In a word, Margaret fell back upon the extreme cynicism and world-weariness of twenty-three, and assured herself that she despised everybody, whereas, as a matter of fact, she never in her life succeeded in disliking anything except mice and piano-practice, and, for a very little while, Billy Woods; and this for the very excellent reason that the gods had fashioned her solely to the end that she might love all mankind, and in return be loved by humanity in general and adored by that portion of it which inhabits trousers.

But, "The rats always desert a sinking ship," said Miss Hugonin, with the air of one delivering a particularly original sentiment. "They make me awfully tired, and I don't care for them in the least. But Petheridge Jukesbury is a *dear*, and I may be poor now, but I *did* try to do good with the money when I had it, and *anyhow*, Billy is going to get well."

And, after all, that was the one thing that really mattered, though of course Billy would always despise her. He would be quite right, too, the girl thought humbly.

But the conventionalities of life are more powerful than even youthful cynicism and youthful heart-break. Prior to devoting herself to a loveless life and the commonplaces of the stoic's tub, Miss Hugonin was compelled by the barest decency to bid her guests Godspeed.

And Adèle Haggage kissed her for the first time in her life. She had been a little awed by Miss Hugonin, the famous heiress—a little jealous of her, I dare say, on account of Hugh Van Orden—but now she kissed her very heartily in farewell, and said, "Don't forget you are to come to us as soon as *possible*," and was beyond any question perfectly sincere in saying it.

And Hugh Van Orden almost dragged Margaret under the main stairway, and, far from showing any marked abhorrence to her in her present state of destitution, implored her with tears in his eyes to marry him at once, and to bring the Colonel to live with them for the rest of his natural existence.

For, "It's damned impertinent of me, of course," Mr. Van Orden readily conceded, "and I suppose I ought to beg your pardon for mentioning it, but I *do* love you to a perfectly unlimited extent. It's playing the very deuce with my polo, Miss Hugonin, and as for my appetite—why, if you won't have me," cried Hugh, in desperation, "I—I really, you know, I don't believe I'll *ever* be able to eat anything!"

When Margaret refused him—for the sixth time, I think—I won't swear that she didn't kiss him under the dark stairway. And if she did, he was a nice boy, and he deserved it.

And as for Sarah Ellen Haggage, that unreverend old parasite brought her a blank cheque signed with her name, and mentioned quite a goodly sum as the extent to which Margaret might go for necessary expenses.

"For you'll need it," she said, and rubbed her nose reflectively. "Moving is the very deuce for wasting money, because so many little things keep cropping up. Now, remember, a quarter is quite enough to give *any* man for moving a trunk. And there's no earthly sense in your taking a cab, Margaret—the street-car will bring you within a block of our door. These little trifles count, dear. And don't let Célestine pack your things, because she's abominably careless. Let Marie do it—and don't tip her. Give her an old hat. And if I were you, I would certainly consult a lawyer about the legality of that idiotic will. I remember distinctly hearing that Mr. Woods was very eccentric in his last days, and I haven't a doubt he was raving mad when, he left all his money to a great, strapping, long-legged young fellow, who is perfectly capable of taking care of himself. Getting better, is he? Well, I suppose I'm glad to hear it, but he'd much better have stayed in Paris—where, I remember distinctly hearing, he led the most dissipated and immoral life, my dear—instead of coming over here and upsetting everything." And again Mrs. Haggage rubbed her nose—indignantly.

"He *didn't*!" said Margaret. "And I *can't* take your money, beautiful! And I don't see how we can possibly come to stay with you."

"Don't you argue with me!" Mrs. Haggage exhorted her. "I'm not in any temper to be argued with. I've spent the morning sewing bias stripes in a bias skirt—something which from a moral-ruining and resolution-overthrowing standpoint simply knocks the spots off Job. You'll take that money, and you'll come to me as soon as you can, and—God bless you, my dear!"

And again Margaret was kissed. Altogether, it was a very osculatory morning for Miss Hugonin.

Mr. Jukesbury's adieus, however, were more formal; and—I am sorry to say it—the old fellow went away wondering if the rich Mr. Woods might not conceivably be very grateful to the man who had saved his life and evince his gratitude in some agreeable and substantial form.

Mrs. Saumarez and Mr. Kennaston, also, were somewhat unenthusiastic in their parting. Kennaston could not feel quite at ease with Margaret, brazen it as he might with devil-may-carish flippancy; and Kathleen had by this an inkling as to how matters stood between Margaret and Billy, and was somewhat puzzled thereat, and loved the former in consequence no more than any Christian female is compelled to love the woman who, either unconsciously or with deliberation, purloins her ancient lover. A woman rarely forgives the man who has ceased to care for her; and rarelier still can she pardon the woman who has dared succeed her in his affections.

And besides, they were utterly engrossed with one another, and utterly happy, and utterly selfish with the immemorial selfishness of lovers, who cannot for a moment conceive that the whole world is not somehow benefited by their happiness and does not await with breathless interest the outcome of their bickerings with the blind bow-god, and from this providential delusion derive a meritorious and comfortable glow. So Mrs. Saumarez and Mr. Kennaston parted from Margaret with kindness, it is true, but not without awkwardness.

And that was the man that almost she had loved! thought Margaret, as she gazed on the whirl of dust left by their carriage-wheels. Gone with a few perfunctory words of sympathy!

And for my part, I think that the base Indian who threw a pearl away worth more than all his tribe was, in comparison with Felix Kennaston, a shrewd and long-headed man. If you had given *me* his chances, Margaret. . . but this, however, is highly digressive.

The Colonel, standing beside her, used language that was unrefined. His aspirations as to the future of Mr. Kennaston and Mr. Jukesbury, it appeared, were both lurid and unfriendly.

"But why, attractive?" queried his daughter.

"May they be qualified with such and such adjectives!" desired the Colonel, fervently. "They tried to lend me money—wouldn't hear of my not taking it! In case of necessity.' Bah!" said the Colonel, and shook his fist after the retreating carriages. "May they be qualified with such and such adjectives!"

How happily she laughed! "And you're swearing at them!" she pouted. "Oh, my dear, my dear, how hard you are on all my little friends!"

"Of course I am," said the Colonel, stoutly. "They've deprived me of the pleasure of despising 'em. It was worth double the money, I tell you! I never objected to any men quite so much. And now they've gone and behaved decently with the deliberate purpose of annoying me! Oh!" cried the Colonel, and shook an immaculate, withered old hand toward the spring sky, "may they be qualified with such and such adjectives!"

And that, so far as we are concerned, was the end of Margaret's satellites.

My dear Mrs. Grundy, may one point the somewhat obvious moral? I thank you, madam, for your long-suffering kindness. Permit me, then, to vault toward my moral over the shoulders of a greater man.

Among the papers left by one Charles Dickens—a novelist who is obsolete now because he "wallows naked in the pathetic" and was frequently guilty of a very vulgar sort of humour that actually made people laugh, which, as we now know, is not the purpose of humour—a novelist who incessantly "caricatured Nature" and by these inartistic and underhand methods created characters that are more real to us than the folk we jostle in the street and (God knows!) far more vital and worthy of attention than the folk who "cannot read Dickens"—you will find, I say, a note of an idea which he never afterward developed, running to this effect: "Full length portrait of his lordship, surrounded by worshippers. Sensible men enough, agreeable men enough, independent men enough in a certain way; but the moment they begin to circle round my lord, and to shine with a borrowed light from his lordship, heaven and earth, how mean and subservient! What a competition and outbidding of each other in servility!"

And this, with "my lord" and "his lordship" erased to make way for the word "money," is my moral. The folk who have just left Selwoode were honest enough as honesty goes nowadays; kindly as any of us dare be who have our own way to make among very stalwart and determined rivals; generous as any man may venture to be in a world where the first of every month finds the butcher and the baker and the candlestick-maker rapping at the door with their little bills: but they cringed to money. It was very wrong of them, my dear lady, and in extenuation I can only plead that they could no more help cringing to money than you or I can help it.

This is very crude and very cynical, but unfortunately it is true.

We always cringe to money; which is humiliating. And the sun always rises at an hour when sensible people are abed and have not the least need for its services; which is foolish. And what you and I, my dear madam, are to do about rectifying either one of these vexatious circumstances, I am sure I don't know.

We can, at least, be honest. Let us, then, console ourselves at will with moral observations concerning the number of pockets in a shroud and the difficulty of a rich man's entering into the kingdom of Heaven; but with an humble and reverent heart, let us admit that, in the world we know, money rules. Its presence awes us. And if we are quite candid we must concede that we very unfeignedly envy and admire the rich; we must grant that money confers a certain distinction on a man, be he the veriest ass that ever heehawed a platitude, and that we cannot but treat him accordingly, you and I.

You are friendly, of course, with your poor cousins; you are delighted to have them drop in to dinner, and liberal enough with the claret when they do; but when the magnate comes, there is a magnum of champagne, and an extra lamp in the drawing-room, and—I blush to write it—a far more agreeable hostess at the head of the table. Dives is such good company, you see. And speaking for my own sex, I defy any honest fellow to lay his hand upon his waistcoat and swear that it doesn't give him a distinct thrill of pleasure to be seen in public with a millionaire. Daily we truckle in the Eagle's shadow—the shadow that lay so heavily across Selwoode. With the Eagle himself and with the Eagle's work in the world—the grim, implacable, ruthless work that hourly he goes about—our little comedy has naught to do; Schlemihl-like, we deal but in shadows. Even the shadow of the Eagle is a terrible thing—a shadow that, as Felix Kennaston has told you, chills faith, and charity, and independence, and kindliness, and truth, and—alas—even common honesty.

But this is both cynical and digressive.

Chapter 31

D r. Jeal, better than his word, had Billy Woods out of bed in five days. To Billy they were very long and very dreary days, and to Margaret very long and penitential ones. But Colonel Hugonin enjoyed them thoroughly; for, as he feelingly and frequently observed, it is an immense consolation to any man to reflect that his home no longer contains "more damn' foolishness to the square inch than any other house in the United States."

On all sides they sought for Cock-eye Flinks. But they never found him, and to this day they have never found him. The Fates having played their pawn, swept it from the board, and Cock-eye Flinks disappeared in Clotho's capacious pocket.

All this time the young people saw nothing of one another. On this point Jeal was adamantean.

"In a sick-room," he vehemently declared, "a woman is well enough, but *the* woman is the devil and all. I've told that young man plainly, sir, that he doesn't see your daughter till he gets well—and, by George, sir, he'll get well now just in order to see her. Nature is the only doctor who ever cures anybody, Colonel; we humans, for all our pill-boxes and lancets, can only prompt her—and devilish demoralising advice we generally give her, too," he added, with a chuckle.

"Peggy!"

This was the first observation of Mr. Woods when he came to his senses. He swore feebly when Peggy was denied to him. He pleaded. He scolded. He even threatened, as a last resort, to get out of bed and go in immediate search of her; and in return, Jeal told him very affably that it was far less difficult to manage a patient in a straight-jacket than one out of it, and that personally nothing would please him so much as a plausible pretext for clapping Mr. Woods into one of 'em. Jeal had his own methods in dealing with the fractious.

Then Billy clamoured for Colonel Hugonin, and subsequently the Colonel came in some bewilderment to his daughter's rooms.

"Billy says that will ain't to be probated," he informed her, testily. "I'm to make sure it ain't probated till he gets well. You're to give me your word you'll do nothing further in the matter till Billy gets well. That's his message, and I'd like to know what the devil this infernal nonsense means. I ain't a Fenian nor yet a Guy Fawkes, daughter, and in consequence I'm free to confess I don't care for all this damn mystery and shilly-shallying. But that's the message."

Miss Hugonin debated with herself. "That I will do nothing further in the matter till Billy gets well," she repeated, reflectively. "Yes, I suppose I'll have to promise it, but you can tell him for me that I consider he is *horrid*, and just as obstinate and selfish as he can *possibly* be. Can you remember that, attractive?"

"Yes, thank you," said the Colonel. "I can remember it, but I ain't going to. Nice sort of message to send a sick man, ain't it? I don't know what's gotten into you, Margaret—no, begad, I don't! I think you're possessed of seventeen devils. And now," the old gentleman demanded, after an awkward pause, "are you or are you not going to tell me what all this mystery is about?"

"I can't," Miss Hugonin protested. "It—it's a secret, attractive."

"It ain't," said the Colonel, flatly—"it's some more damn foolishness." And he went away in a fret and using language.

Chapter 32

L eft to herself, Miss Hugonin meditated.

Miss Hugonin was in her kimono.

And oh, Madame Chrysastheme! oh, Madame Butterfly! Oh, Mimosa San, and Pitti Sing, and Yum Yum, and all ye vaunted beauties of Japan! if you could have seen her in that garb! Poor little ladies of the Orient, how hopelessly you would have wrung your henna-stained fingers! Poor little Ichabods of the East, whose glory departed irretrievably when she adopted this garment, I tremble to think of the heart-burnings and palpitations and hari-karis that would have ensued.

It was pink—the pink of her cheeks to a shade. And scattered about it were birds, and butterflies, and snaky, emaciated dragons, with backs like saw-teeth, and prodigious fangs, and claws, and very curly tails, such as they breed in Nankeen plates and used to breed on packages of fire-crackers—all done in gold, the gold of her hair. Moreover, one might catch a glimpse of her neck—which was a manifest favour of the gods—and about it mysterious, lacy white things intermingling with divers tiny blue ribbons. I saw her in it once—by accident.

And now I fancy, as she stood rigid with indignation, her cheeks flushed, it must have been a heady spectacle to note how their shell-pink repeated the pink of her fantastic garment like a chromatic echo; and how her sunny hair, a thought loosened, a shade dishevelled, clung heavily about her face, a golden snare for eye and heart; and how her own eyes, enormous, cerulean—twin sapphires such as in the old days might have ransomed a brace of emperors—grew wistful like a child's who has been punished and does not know exactly why; and how her petulant mouth quivered and the long black lashes, golden at the roots, quivered, too—ah, yes, it must have been a heady spectacle.

"*Now*," she announced, "I see plainly what he intends doing. He is going to destroy that will, and burden me once more with a large and influential fortune. I don't want it, and I won't take it, and he might just as well understand that in the very beginning. I don't care if Uncle Fred did leave it to me—I didn't ask him to, did I? Besides, he was a very foolish old man—if he had left the money to Billy *everything* would have been all right. That's always the way—my dolls are invariably stuffed with sawdust, and I *never* have a dear gazelle to glad me with his dappled hide, but when he comes to know me well he falls upon the buttered side—or something to that effect. I hate poetry, anyhow—it's so mushy!"

And this from the Miss Hugonin who a week ago was interested in the French *decadents* and partial to folk-songs from the Romaic! I think we may fairly deduce that the reign of Felix Kennaston is over. The king is dead; and Margaret's thoughts and affections and her very dreams have fallen loyally to crying, Long live the king—his Majesty Billy the First.

"Oh!" said Margaret, with an indignant gasp, what time her eyebrows gesticulated, "I think Billy Woods is a meddlesome *piece*!—that's what I think! Does he suppose that after waiting all this time for the only man in the world who can keep me interested for four hours on a stretch and send my pulse up to a hundred and make me feel those thrilly thrills I've always longed for—does he suppose that now I'm going to pay any attention to his silly notions about wills and things? He's abominably selfish! I shan't!"

Margaret moved across the room, shimmering, rustling, glittering like a fairy in a pantomime. Then, to consider matters at greater ease, she curled up on a divan in much the attitude of a tiny Cleopatra riding at anchor on a carpeted Cydnus.

"Billy thinks I want the money—bless his boots! He thinks I'm a stuck-up, grasping, purse-proud little pig, and he has every right to think so after the way I talked to him, though he ought to have realised I was in a temper about Kathleen Saumarez and have paid no attention to what I said. And he actually attempted to reason with me! If he'd had *any* consideration for my feelings, he'd have simply smacked me and made me behave—however, he's a man, and all men are selfish, and *she's* a skinny old thing, and I *never* had any use for her. Bother her lectures! I never understood a word of them, and I don't believe she does, either. Women's clubs are *all* silly, and I think the women who belong to them are *all* bold-faced jigs! If they had any sense, they'd stay at home and take care of the babies, instead of messing with philanthropy, and education, and theosophy, and anything else that they can't make head or tail of. And they call that being cultured! Culture!—I hate the word! I don't want to be cultured—I want to be happy."

This, you will observe, was, in effect, a sweeping recantation of every ideal Margaret had ever boasted. But Love is a canny pedagogue, and of late he had instructed Miss Hugonin in a variety of matters.

"Before God, loving you as I do, I wouldn't marry you for all the wealth in the world," she repeated, with a little shiver. "Even in his delirium he said that. But I *know* now that he loves me. And I know that I adore him. And if this were a sensible world, I'd walk right in there and explain things and ask him to marry me, and then it wouldn't matter in the least who had the money. But I can't, because it wouldn't be proper. Bother propriety!—but bothering it doesn't do any good. As long as I have the money, Billy will never come near me, because of the idiotic way I talked to him. And he's bent on my taking the money simply because it happens to belong to me. I consider that a very silly reason. I'll *make* Billy Woods take the money, and I'll make him see that I'm *not* a little pig, and that I trust him implicitly. And I think I'm quite justified in using a little— we'll call it diplomacy—because otherwise he'd go back to France or some other objectionable place, and we'd both be *very* unhappy."

Margaret began to laugh softly. "I've given him my word that I'll do nothing further in the matter till he gets well. And I won't. *But——*"

Miss Hugonin rose from the divan with a gesture of sweeping back her hair. And then—oh, treachery of tortoise-shell! oh, the villainy of those little gold hair-pins!—the fat twisted coils tumbled loose and slowly unravelled themselves, and her pink-and-white face, half-eclipsed, showed a delectable wedge between big, odourful, crinkly, ponderous masses of hair. It clung about her, a heavy cloak, all shimmering gold like the path of sunset over the June sea. And Margaret, looking at herself in the mirror, laughed, and appeared perfectly content with what she saw there.

"But," said she, "if the Fates are kind to me—and I sometimes think I *have* a pull with the gods—I'll make you happy, Billy Woods, in spite of yourself."

The mirror flashed back a smile. Margaret was strangely interested in the mirror.

"She has ringlets in her hair," sang Margaret happily—a low, half-hushed little song. She held up a strand of it to demonstrate this fact.

"There's a dimple in her chin"—and, indeed, there was. And a dimple in either cheek, too.

For a long time afterward she continued to smile at the mirror. I am afraid Kathleen Saumarez was right. She was a vain little cat, was Margaret.

But, barring a rearrangement of the cosmic scheme, I dare say maids will continue to delight in their own comeliness so long as mirrors speak truth. Let us, then, leave Miss Hugonin to this innocent diversion. The staidest of us are conscious of a brisk elation at sight of a pretty face; and surely no considerate person will deny its owner a portion of the pleasure that daily she accords the beggar at the street-corner.

JAMES BRANCH CABELL

Chapter 33

We are credibly informed that Time travels in divers paces with divers persons—the statement being made by a lady who may be considered to speak with some authority, having triumphantly withstood the ravages of Chronos for a matter of three centuries. But I doubt if even the insolent sweet wit of Rosalind could have devised a fitting simile for Time's gait at Selwoode those five days that Billy lay abed. Margaret could not but marvel at the flourishing proportion attained by the hours in those sunlit spring days; and at dinner, say, her thoughts harking back to luncheon, recalled it by a vigorous effort as an affair of the dim yester-years—a mere blurred memory, faint and vague as a Druidical tenet or a Merovingian squabble.

But the time passed for all that; and eventually—it was just before dusk—she came, with Martin Jeal's permission, into the room where Billy was. And beside the big open fireplace, where a wood fire chattered companionably, sat a very pallid Billy, a rather thin Billy, with a great many bandages about his head.

You may depend upon it, Margaret was not looking her worst that afternoon. By actual count, Célestine had done her hair six times before reaching an acceptable result.

And, "Yes, Célestine, you may get out that pale yellow dress. No, beautiful, the one with the black satin stripes on the bodice—because I don't want my hair cast completely in the shade, do I? Now, let me see—black feather, gloves, large pompadour, *and* a sweet smile. No, I don't want a fan—that's a Lydia Languish trade-mark. And *two* silk skirts rustling like the deadest leaves imaginable. Yes, I think that will do. And if you can't hook up my dress without pecking and pecking at me like that, I'll probably go stark, *staring* crazy, Célestine, and then you'll be sorry. No, it isn't a bit tight—are you perfectly certain there's no powder behind my ears, Célestine? Now, *please* try to fasten the collar without pulling all my hair down. Ye-es, I think that will do, Célestine. Well, it's very nice of you to say so, but I don't believe I much fancy myself in yellow, after all."

Equipped and armed for conquest, then, she came into the room with a very tolerable affectation of unconcern. Altogether, it was a quite effective entrance.

"I've been for a little drive, Billy," she mendaciously informed him. "That's how you happen to have the opportunity of seeing me in all my nice new store-clothes. Aren't you pleased, Billy? No, don't you dare get up!" Margaret stood across the room, peeling off her gloves and regarding him on the whole with disapproval. "They've been starving you," she pensively reflected. "As soon as that Jeal person goes away, I shall have six little beefsteaks cooked and see to it personally that you eat every one of them. And I'll cook a cherry pie—quick as a cat can wink her eye—won't I, Billy? That Jeal person is a decided nuisance," said Miss Hugonin, as she stabbed her hat rather viciously with two hat-pins and then laid it aside on a table.

Billy Woods was looking up at her forlornly. It hurt her to see the love and sorrow in his face. But oh, how avidly his soul drank in the modulations of that longed-for voice—a voice that was honey and gold and velvet and all that is most sweet and rich and soft in the world.

"Peggy," said he, plunging at the heart of things, "where's that will?"

Miss Hugonin kicked forward a little foot-stool to the other side of the fire, and sat down and complacently smoothed out her skirts.

"I knew it!" said she. "I never saw such a one-idea'd person in my life. I knew that would be the very first thing you would ask for, Billy Woods, because you're such an obstinate, stiffnecked *donkey*. Very well!"—and Margaret tossed her head—"here's Uncle Fred's will, then, and you can do *exactly* as you like with it, and *now* I hope you're satisfied!" And Margaret handed him the long envelope which lay in her lap.

Mr. Woods promptly opened it.

"That," Miss Hugonin commented, "is what I term very unladylike behaviour on your part."

"You evidently don't trust me, Billy Woods. Very well! I don't care! Read it carefully—very carefully, and make quite sure I haven't been dabbling in forgery of late—besides, it's so good for your eyes, you know, after being hit over the head," Margaret suggested, cheerfully.

Billy chuckled. "That's true," said he, "but I know Uncle Fred's fist well enough without having to read it all. Candidly, Peggy, I *had* to look at it, because I—well, I didn't quite trust you, Peggy. And now we're going to burn this interesting paper, you and I." "Wait!" Margaret cried. "Ah, wait, just a moment, Billy!"

He glanced up at her in surprise, the paper still poised in his hand.

She sat with head drooped forward, her masculine little chin thrust out eagerly, her candid eyes transparently appraising him.

"Why are you going to burn it, Billy?"

"Why?" Mr. Woods, repeated, thoughtfully. "Well, for a variety of reasons. First is, that Uncle Fred really did leave his money to you, and burning this is the only way of making sure you get it. Why, I thought you wanted me to burn it! Last time I saw you—"

"I was in a temper," said Margaret, haughtily. "You ought to have seen that."

"Yes, I—er—noticed it," Mr. Woods admitted, with some dryness; "but it wasn't only temper. You've grown accustomed to the money. You'd miss it now—miss the pleasure it gives you, miss the power it gives you. You'd never be content to go back to the old life now. Why, Peggy, you yourself told me you thought money the greatest thing in the world! It has changed you, Peggy, this—ah, well!" said Billy, "we won't talk about that. I'm going to burn it because that's the only honourable thing to do. Ready, Peggy?"

"It may be honourable, but it's *extremely* silly," Margaret temporised, "and for my part, I'm very, very glad God had run out of a sense of honour when He created the woman."

"Phrases don't alter matters. Ready, Peggy?"

"Ah, no, phrases don't alter matters!" she assented, with a quick lift of speech. "You're going to destroy that will, Billy Woods, simply because you think I'm a horrid, mercenary, selfish *pig*. You think I couldn't give up the money—you think I couldn't be happy without it. Well, you have every right to think so, after the way I've behaved. But why not tell me that is the real reason?"

Billy raised his hand in protest. "I—I think you might miss it," he conceded. "Yes, I think you would miss it."

"Listen!" said Margaret, quickly. "The money is yours now—by my act. You say you—care for me. If I am the sort of woman you think me—I don't say I am, and I don't say I'm not—but thinking me that sort of woman, don't you think I'd—I'd marry you for the asking if you kept the money? Don't you think you're losing every chance of me by burning that will? Oh, I'm not standing on conventionalities now! Don't you think that, Billy?"

She was tempting him to the uttermost; and her heart was sick with fear lest he might yield. This was the Eagle's last battle; and recreant Love fought with the Eagle against poor Billy, who had only his honour to help him.

Margaret's face was pale as she bent toward him, her lips parted a little, her eyes glinting eerily in the firelight. The room was dark now save in the small radius of its amber glow; beyond that was darkness where panels and brasses blinked.

"Yes," said Billy, gravely—"forgive me if I'm wrong, dear, but—I do think that. But you see you don't care for me, Peggy. In the summer-house I thought for a moment—ah, well, you've shown in a hundred ways that you don't care—and I wouldn't have you come to me, not caring. So I'm going to burn the paper, dear."

Margaret bowed her head. Had she ever known happiness before?

"It is not very flattering to me," she said, "but it shows that you— care—a great deal. You care enough to—let me go. Ah—yes. You may burn it now, Billy."

And promptly he tossed it into the flames. For a moment it lay unharmed; then the edges caught and crackled and blazed, and their heads drew near together as they watched it burn.

There (thought Billy) is the end! Ah, ropes, daggers, and poisons! there is the end! Oh, Peggy. Peggy, if you could only have loved me! if only this accursed money hadn't spoiled you so utterly! Billy was quite properly miserable over it.

But he raised his head with a smile. "And now," said he—and not without a little, little bitterness; "if I have any right to advise you, Peggy, I—I think I'd be more careful in the future as to how I used the money. You've tried to do good with it, I know. But every good cause has its parasites. Don't trust entirely to the Haggages and Jukesburys, Peggy, and—and don't desert the good ship Philanthropy because there are a few barnacles on it, dear."

"You make me awfully tired," Miss Hugonin observed, as she rose to her feet. "How do you suppose I'm going to do anything for Philanthropy or any other cause when I haven't a penny in the world? You see, you've just burned the last will Uncle Fred ever made—the one that left everything to me. The one in your favour was probated or proved or whatever they call it a week ago." I think Billy was surprised.

She stood over him, sharply outlined against the darkness, clasping her hands tightly just under her chin, ludicrously suggestive of a pre-Raphaelitish saint. In the firelight her hair was an aureole; and her gown, yellow with multitudinous tiny arabesques of black velvet, echoed the glow of her hair to a shade. The dancing flames made of her a flickering little yellow wraith. And oh, the quaint tenderness of her eyes!—oh, the hint of faint, nameless perfume she diffused! thus ran the meditations of Billy's dizzied brain.

"Listen! I told you I burned the other will. I started to burn it. But I was afraid to, because I didn't know what they could do to me if I did.

So I put it away in my little handkerchief-box—and if you'd had a *grain* of sense you'd have noticed the orris on it. And you made me promise not to take any steps in the matter till you got well. I knew you would. So I had already sent that second will—sent it before I promised you— to Hunston Wyke—he's my lawyer now, you know—and I've heard from him, and he has probated it."

Billy was making various irrelevant sounds.

"And I brought that other will to you, and if you didn't choose to examine it more carefully I'm sure it wasn't my fault. I kept my word like a perfect gentleman and took no step *whatever* in the matter. I didn't say a word when before my eyes you stripped me of my entire worldly possessions—you know I didn't. You burned it up yourself, Billy Woods—of your own free will and accord—and now Selwoode and all that detestable money belongs to *you*, and I'm sure I'd like to know what you are going to do about it. So *there!*"

Margaret faced him defiantly. Billy was in a state of considerable perturbation.

"Why have you done this?" he asked, slowly. But a lucent something— half fear, half gladness—was wakening in Billy's eyes.

And her eyes answered him. But her tongue was far less veracious.

"Because you thought I was a *pig*! Because you couldn't make allowances for a girl who for four years has seen nothing but money and money-worshippers and the power of money! Because I wanted your—your respect, Billy. And you thought I couldn't give it up! Very well!" Miss Hugonin waved her hand airily toward the hearth. "Now I hope you know better. *Don't you dare get up, Billy Woods!*"

But I think nothing short of brute force could have kept Mr. Woods from her.

"Peggy," he babbled—"ah, forgive me if I'm a presumptuous ass—but was it because you knew I couldn't ask you to marry me so long as you had the money?"

She dallied with her bliss. Margaret was on the other side of the table.

"Why—why, of course it wasn't!" she panted. "What nonsense!"

"Look at me, Peggy!"

"I don't want to! You look like a fright with your head all tied up."

"Peggy. . . this exercise is bad for an invalid."

"I—oh, please sit down! *Please*, Billy! It is bad for you."

"Not until you tell me——"

"But I *don't!*. . . Oh, you make me *awfully* tired."

"Peggy, don't you dare stamp your foot at me!. . . Peggy!"

"*Please* sit down! Now. . . well, there's my hand, stupid, if you *will* be silly. Now sit down here—so, with your head leaned back on this nice little cushion because it's good for your poor head—and I'll sit on this nice little footstool and be quite, quite honest. No, you must lean back—I don't care if you can't see me, I'd much rather you couldn't. Well, the truth is—no, you *must* lean back—the truth is—I've loved you all my life, Billy Woods, and—no, not *yet*, Billy—and if you hadn't been the stupidest beautiful in the universe you'd have seen it long ago. You—you needn't—lean back—any longer, Billy. . . Oh, Billy, why *didn't* you shave?"

"She *is* skinny, isn't she, Billy?"

"Now, Peggy, you mustn't abuse Kathleen. She's a friend of mine."

"Well, I know she's a friend of yours, but that doesn't prevent her being skinny, does it?"

"Now, Peggy—"

"Please, Billy! *Please* say she's skinny!"

"Er—well, she's a bit thin, perhaps."

"You angel!"

"And you're quite sure you've forgiven me for doubting you?"

"And you've forgiven *me?*"

"Bless you, Peggy, I never doubted you! I've been too busy loving you."

"It seems to me as if it had been—*always*."

"Why, didn't we love one another in Carthage, Peggy?"

"I think it was in Babylon, Billy."

"And will love one another——?"

"Forever and ever, dear. You've been to seek a wife, Billy boy."

"And oh, the dimple in her chin. . ."

Ah, well! There was a deal of foolish prattle there in the firelight— delectable prattle, irresponsible as the chattering of birds after a storm. And I fancy that the Eagle's shadow is lifted from Selwoode, now that Love has taken up his abode there.

The End

A Note About the Author

James Branch Cabell (1879–1958) was an American writer of escapist and fantasy fiction. Born into a wealthy family in the state of Virginia, Cabell attended the College of William and Mary, where he graduated in 1898 following a brief personal scandal. His first stories began to be published, launching a productive decade in which Cabell's worked appeared in both *Harper's Monthly Magazine* and *The Saturday Evening Post*. Over the next forty years, Cabell would go on to publish fifty-two books, many of them novels and short-story collections. A friend, colleague, and inspiration for such writers as Ellen Glasgow, H.L. Mencken, Sinclair Lewis, and Theodore Dreiser, James Branch Cabell is remembered as an iconoclastic pioneer of fantasy literature.

A Note from the Publisher

Spanning many genres, from non-fiction essays to literature classics to children's books and lyric poetry, Mint Edition books showcase the master works of our time in a modern new package. The text is freshly typeset, is clean and easy to read, and features a new note about the author in each volume. Many books also include exclusive new introductory material. Every book boasts a striking new cover, which makes it as appropriate for collecting as it is for gift giving. Mint Edition books are only printed when a reader orders them, so natural resources are not wasted. We're proud that our books are never manufactured in excess and exist only in the exact quantity they need to be read and enjoyed.

bookfinity™

Discover more of your favorite classics with Bookfinity™.

- Track your reading with custom book lists.
- Get great book recommendations for your personalized Reader Type.
- Add reviews for your favorite books.
- AND MUCH MORE!

Visit **bookfinity.com** and take the fun Reader Type quiz to get started.

Enjoy our classic and modern companion pairings!

Classic & Modern